D0540689

Maybe his whole life had been building to this kiss.

It was a crazy thing to think—but how could he think it was crazy when his hands were cupping her face and he was drawing her in to meet him? How could he think he was crazy when his mouth was lowering to hers and she was so sweet, so beautiful, so right?

She wanted him. He felt her need and his whole body responded. Their kiss was suddenly urgent, hard, demanding. It was as if a magnetic field had been created, locking them to each other, two force fields meeting, as they must, with fire at the centre.

He wanted her. He felt…out of control. Maybe he *was* out of control. It was Christmas Eve. He was with a woman he'd thought he'd known but now realised he hadn't known at all.

His Meg.

Dear Reader

Sigh. As I write this, Christmas is over for another year, and there's a mixture of relief and regret as I pack up the decorations. I can still hear my grandma muttering, 'It's not worth packing them up. It comes round so fast that before you know it you'll be pulling them out again.' And of course Grandma's right, but from here it seems a long time 'til I get my next hit of Santa Clausing, carols and eggnog.

Anyway, just to keep me going until next year, I've indulged in the next best thing to Christmas, which is a Christmas romance for you to enjoy as you take the decorations out again. My story has all my favourite things: a hero to die for, drama, fun, dogs, cows, a birth—oh, and did I mention eggnog?

I loved locking my heroine on her farm with her to-die-for boss. A billionaire boss—what greater gift could a girl find in her stocking on Christmas morning?

Enjoy!

Marion Lennox

CHRISTMAS WITH HER BOSS

BY
MARION LENNOX

All the characters in this book have no existence outside the imagination of the author, and have no relation whatsoever to anyone bearing the same name or names. They are not even distantly inspired by any individual known or unknown to the author, and all the incidents are pure invention.

All Rights Reserved including the right of reproduction in whole or in part in any form. This edition is published by arrangement with Harlequin Enterprises II BV/S.à.r.l. The text of this publication or any part thereof may not be reproduced or transmitted in any form or by any means, electronic or mechanical, including photocopying, recording, storage in an information retrieval system, or otherwise, without the written permission of the publisher.

® and TM are trademarks owned and used by the trademark owner and/or its licensee. Trademarks marked with ® are registered with the United Kingdom Patent Office and/or the Office for Harmonisation in the Internal Market and in other countries.

First published in Great Britain 2010
Harlequin Mills & Boon Limited,
Eton House, 18-24 Paradise Road, Richmond, Surrey TW9 1SR

© Marion Lennox 2010

ISBN: 978 0 263 21537 3

Harlequin Mills & Boon policy is to use papers that are natural, renewable and recyclable products and made from wood grown in sustainable forests. The logging and manufacturing process conform to the legal environmental regulations of the country of origin.

Printed and bound in Great Britain
by CPI Antony Rowe, Chippenham, Wiltshire

Marion Lennox is a country girl, born on an Australian dairy farm. She moved on—mostly because the cows just weren't interested in her stories! Married to a 'very special doctor', Marion writes Mills & Boon® Medical™ Romances as well as Mills & Boon® Romance (she used a different name for each category for a while—if you're looking for her past romances search for author Trisha David as well). She's now had over 75 romance novels accepted for publication.

In her non-writing life Marion cares for kids, cats, dogs, chooks and goldfish. She travels, she fights her rampant garden (she's losing), and her house dust (she's lost).

Having spun in circles for the first part of her life, she's now stepped back from her 'other' career, which was teaching statistics at her local university. Finally she's reprioritised her life, figured what's important and discovered the joys of deep baths, romance and chocolate.

Preferably all at the same time!

MORAY COUNCIL LIBRARIES & INFO.SERVICES	
20 31 05 77	
Askews	
RF RF	

CHAPTER ONE

'ALL scheduled flights have been cancelled until after Christmas. Charter planes are no exception. I'm sorry, ma'am, but nobody's going anywhere.'

Meg replaced the phone as if it was about to shatter. The air around her felt sharp and dangerous. She was trying hard not to breathe.

The door to her boss's inner sanctum was open. W S McMaster was clearing his desk, filing vital documents into his lovely calfskin briefcase. Suave, sleek and almost impossibly good-looking, the man looked what he was—a billionaire businessman moving on to the next important thing.

But the next important thing was in New York, and W S McMaster's personal assistant was about to tell him there were no planes for at least three days.

No-o-o-o-o-o.

'Oh, Meg, I'm so out of here.' Josie, Meg's assistant, was tugging off her office shoes and hauling on six-inch stilettos. 'Dan's meeting me in five minutes and I'm free. How cool to have Christmas fall on Monday. I have two solid days of partying until I need to sober up for the family Christmas Day.'

Meg didn't answer. She couldn't.

Josie and the rest of the office staff departed, calling Christmas greetings as they left. Yes, Christmas was on

Monday. It was Friday afternoon. The corporate world closed down, right now.

Except for Meg, whose job it was to be at hand as Mr McMaster's personal assistant at any time he was in Australia.

Mr McMaster was only in Australia for maybe ten or twelve weeks of the year, and there was little administration she had to do outside those times. It was a fabulous job. She'd been so lucky to get it. If she'd messed this up…

Don't go there. Focus on now. Focus on getting her boss out of the country. She gave a weak little wave to the departing staff and tried one last phone call.

Her boss was too far away to hear, but there was little to hear anyway; just more of the same.

'Helicopters depend on air traffic controllers too?' she asked bleakly. 'No, thank you; I understand. And there's no way the strike can be resolved until after Christmas? Of course I know the whole country closes down from five tonight, but this is vital. Can we…I don't know, take off from a paddock while no one's watching? Island hop to Indonesia and find a flight from there? I'm serious; I'll do anything.'

No and no and no.

She replaced her phone and stared at it as if it had person-ally betrayed her—and Mr McMaster was standing in the doorway, ready to go.

He looked ready to take on the world.

He always did, she conceded. William McMaster was thirty-six years old; he'd been born into money and he'd in-herited the gene for making it. He headed a huge family cor-poration and the McMaster empire was growing by the day. For the last three years he'd spent two or three months a year here, growing the part of the firm that was opening mines all over Australia. He flew from one business meeting to another. While he was in Australia Meg flew with him, and as she did she realised why he had a different PA in every country. He'd wear one out in weeks.

She was worn out now, and he was ready to leave. He was leaning against the door, waiting for her attention. He was wearing a dark Italian business suit that screamed money and taste, with a crisp white shirt, new on this morning because the hotel laundry had sent his shirts back slightly yellowed. She'd had a frantic scramble to get new ones. His hotel was supposed to be the best in Melbourne—how could she top that? The hotel also had the best gym in Melbourne. He insisted on hotels with great gyms and his body proved it. Tall, dark, and far more good-looking than any man had a right to be, he was watching her now through dark, hooded eyes, as if he knew something was wrong.

Of course he knew something was wrong. You couldn't get to where he was without intelligence and intuition, and William McMaster had both in spades.

'My car to the airport?' he queried, but softly, as if he already suspected the answer.

'There's a problem,' she said, not looking at him. Her new three year contract was on her desk, waiting for her boss to sign on his way out. She shoved it under her fax, as if somehow hiding it could protect it.

She *so* wanted to keep this job. While Mr McMaster was overseas she wasn't needed, but when he was in the country she moved to total commitment. Seven days out of seven. Twelve hour days, or more.

He worked like this all the time, Meg knew. She was in touch with his three other PAs, one in London, one in New York and one in Hong Kong. Wherever he went, the work of a dozen people followed. The man was driven and he drove everyone around him.

He couldn't drive her now. She *must* go home.

'There's a delay,' Meg managed, trying desperately to sound

as if this was a mere hiccup to be sorted by six. Six, the time his plane took off and she could catch the train home and be free.

He didn't respond. He simply waited, his dark eyes barely flickering. He was a man of few words. He expected his people to anticipate his demands and sort them.

That was what she was paid to do, but this time she'd failed.

She couldn't hire a private jet. Helicopters needed airspace too. How long would it take a boat to get to New Zealand so he could fly from there? A week at least. No.

And hotels… They'd been booked out for months for this holiday weekend. When she'd settled his account this morning the manager already sounded tired in anticipation.

'It's great he's booked out early. I have people queuing. There's not a room to be had in the whole city. I have people offering bribes…'

'Are you intending to tell me?'

His eyes had narrowed—he knew by now that the problem was serious. To her surprise, though, there was a gleam of suppressed amusement in his dark eyes, as if he guessed the mess her thoughts were in.

'There's been a snap strike by air traffic controllers,' she said, feeling ill. 'The conciliation meeting ended twenty minutes ago, with no result. All airlines are grounded indefinitely.'

She could see the airport from this office. Meg snatched a fleeting glance outside. This was the penthouse suite of the most luxurious office block in Melbourne. The view was almost all the way to Tasmania, and normally there were planes between here and the sea.

Now the sky was empty, and her boss's gaze had followed hers.

'No planes,' he said slowly.

'Nothing that needs airspace until after Christmas. There's no guarantee even then. This is…'

'Absurd,' he snapped. 'A private jet…'

'Requires airspace.' She managed to meet his gaze full on. He liked direct answers; hated being messed around. She'd worked with him for three years now and she knew enough not to quail before that steely gaze. Sometimes this man demanded more than was humanly possible. When that happened she told him and he simply moved on.

He wasn't moving on yet.

'Organise me a car to Sydney. I'll fly from there.'

'The strike's Australia-wide.'

'That's impossible. I need to be in New York for Christmas.'

Why? There was enough space in her muddled thoughts to wonder what—or who—was waiting for him at home.

The gossip magazines said this man was a loner. He'd been an only child, and his parents were wealthy to the point of obscenity, long divorced and enmeshed in society living. As far as Meg knew, he never saw them. There'd been an actress on his arm last time he'd been in London but the tabloids had reported her broken heart at least three months ago. And it hadn't been very broken, Meg thought wryly. She knew how much the woman had received during their short relationship— 'Send this to Sarah… Settle Sarah's hotel bill…' and now Sarah had already moved on to the next high-status partner.

So who was waiting in New York?

'I can't get you to New York,' she said, trying to stay calm. To tell it like it was.

'You've tried everything?'

'Yes, sir.'

He stared at her for a long moment and she could see his cool brain assessing the situation. He trusted her—he'd trusted her from the moment he'd hired her—and she could tell by his expression that already he was in Melbourne for Christmas and making the best of it.

'I can work here,' he said, angry but seemingly resigned. Frequent flyers knew that sometimes factors moved out of their control, and she wouldn't be fired for this. 'I'll need to make some fast arrangements, though. We can use the time to sort the Berswood deal. That's urgent enough.'

Deep breath. Just say it.

'Mr McMaster, the Australian corporate world closes down at five this afternoon,' she said, meeting his gaze square on. 'This entire building will be shutting down. There'll be no air conditioning, no servicing; the place will be locked. The business district will be deserted. You pay me to be in charge of this office and I've already let the staff leave. And you can't sort the Berswood contract. There'll be no one at Berswood to sort it with.'

She was meeting her boss's gaze, tilting her chin, trying to sound calmly confident instead of defiant and scared.

She was definitely scared.

McMaster's gaze was almost blank, but she knew there was nothing blank about what he was thinking. This man sorted multi-million business deals in the time it took her to apply lipstick. Not that she had time to apply lipstick when he was around.

'Very well,' he conceded. 'You and I can work from my hotel suite.'

You and I can work from my hotel suite...

Her face must have changed again. He got it. He always knew.

'There's a problem there, too?'

'Sir, there's no rooms.'

'If I have to change hotels I will,' he snapped, but she shook her head. This was why she'd be fired. It was something she should have foreseen. At the first rumour she should have booked, but she'd missed the rumours.

She'd been frantic in the Christmas lead up, and she'd done her shopping in one crazy rush last night. The shops had been open all night. McMaster had let her go at eleven and she'd shopped until three. Then she'd fallen into an exhausted sleep—and been woken to a demand for clean shirts. She'd sorted it and been back in the office at seven, but her normally incisive scheduling had let her down. She'd missed listening to the morning news.

Fallback position… What was that?

There wasn't one.

'There really are no rooms,' she said, as calmly as she could. 'The country's full of trapped people. You left your hotel before seven this morning. Most people book out later. By eight the rumours had started and people simply refused to leave. If I'd figured this out this morning… I didn't and I'm sorry. There's a major Hollywood blockbuster being filmed on location just out of Melbourne. All the cast were due to fly out tonight. They've block-booked every luxury hotel in Melbourne and they're prepared to pay whatever it takes. The cheap places are overwhelmed by groups who can't get home. People are camping at the airport. There really is nothing.'

She hesitated, hating to throw it back to him, knowing she had no choice. 'Sir… Do you have friends? Your parents… There must be people you know?'

There was a moment's loaded silence. Then, 'You're telling me to contact my parents' friends?' The anger in his voice frightened her.

'No, I…'

'There is no way I will contact any friend of my parents— or anyone else. You're suggesting I ask for charity?'

'Of course not, but…'

'To impose myself on someone else's Christmas... I will not.'

'Sir...'

'So, taking away the personal option, where,' he said in a voice that dripped ice, 'do you suggest I stay?'

'I don't know,' she whispered.

'You're paid to know,' he snapped, his face dark with fury. He glanced at his watch. 'You have fifteen minutes. I'll get documents faxed from Berswood to give me work to do over the weekend. Meanwhile, find me something. Somewhere I can work in peace. Now.'

He turned and slammed back into his office and, for the first time in her entire life, Meg felt like having hysterics. Serious hysterics.

Hysterics wouldn't help. Where? Where?

Somewhere he could work in peace?

She could organise a mattress and a sleeping bag here, she thought, feeling more and more out of control. But even this office...without air conditioning...

No. Her job was so ended.

And more... In a little more than an hour, the train to Tandaroit would leave without her. Christmas was waiting. As well as that, there was hay waiting, ready to spoil if it wasn't harvested. She must go home.

She made one more miserable phone call, to a dealer in hotel rooms. Unless she'd take the absolute dregs there was nothing, nothing, nothing.

She sat and stared at her hands until exactly fifteen minutes later, when the door slammed open again.

'Well?' he demanded. His anger was back under control. He was icy calm, waiting for her solution. And there was only one solution to give.

'There are no hotels.'

'So?'

So say it. Just say it.

'So you can come home with me,' she said, trying desperately to make her voice bright and confident. 'It's the only solution, and it's a good one. We have a comfortable private spare room with its own bathroom, and we have the Internet. I'll be on call for your secretarial needs. We can't have you trapped in the city over Christmas. My family and I would be pleased if you could spend Christmas with us.'

If her boss's face had been thunderous before, it was worse now. It was as if there were a live hand-grenade ticking between them. The pin had been pulled. Who knew how long these things took to explode?

'You're offering me charity,' he said at last, slowly, carefully, as if saying the word itself was like taking poison.

'It's not charity at all,' she managed, feeling a faint stirring of anger. 'We'd love to have you.' Oooh, what a lie.

But what was the choice? Sleeping bags here was a real possibility, awful as it seemed. She could spend Christmas trying to make this office liveable, working around a situation which was appalling. Or she could try and resurrect Christmas.

If he accepted, then he'd spend the whole time in his room with his computer, she thought. Thank the stars she'd set up Internet access on the farm. It cost more than she could afford, but it had made Scotty jubilant and maybe…just maybe it would be the decider.

'I do not want to be part of anyone else's Christmas,' he snapped.

'You don't need to be. You can stay in your room and work. I can even bring your meals to your room, if you want to take it that far.'

'I can't believe this is the only solution.'

'It's the only one I can think of.'

No matter what she did, no matter what she offered, she

would lose her job over this, Meg thought miserably, and then she thought—why don't I quit now? She could walk away and leave this man to do whatever he wanted over Christmas.

But this was the best job. And maybe…maybe he'd even enjoy it. Letty put on a great Christmas. Miracles could happen.

Send me a miracle, she pleaded, starting her Santa list right now.

'It will work,' she said, managing to sound much more calm than she felt. 'This is a genuine offer and we'd be very pleased to have you.' She glanced at her watch, acting as if it was time to move on. Acting as if the thing had already been decided. 'You will be able to work. The room has a lovely view.' *Not exactly like this one.* 'You will be comfortable and you will be left alone. If you accept my offer, then my train leaves in an hour. I'm sorry you can't get home but this is the best I can do.'

His face was still dark with fury.

If he was so angry, why didn't he contact someone else? she thought. Any socialite in Melbourne would be pleased to be his friend. He was invited everywhere. Surely he didn't wish to spend Christmas with her.

But it seemed he did.

'Your house is large?'

That was easy. 'Yes, it is.'

'No young children?'

'No.' Scotty was fifteen. Surely that didn't count as young.

'And I will have privacy?'

'Yes, sir.'

'Right,' he said roughly, angrily. 'I'll pay your family for my accommodation and I'll work from there.'

'There's no need to pay.'

'This is business,' he snapped. 'Business or nothing.'

'Fine,' she said, accepting the inevitable. 'I'll get changed. We can walk to the station.'

'Walk?'

'It's Christmas,' she said. 'Traffic's gridlocked and it's four blocks.'

'I will have privacy at this place?' he demanded again, suddenly suspicious.

'At my home,' she said, goaded. 'Yes, you will.'

He hesitated. 'And your family...'

'They'll be glad of the extra income,' she said, knowing that this at least was true.

And it seemed it was the right thing to say. He was moving on.

'Don't think I'm accepting this with any degree of complacency,' he snapped. 'We'll discuss this debacle after Christmas. But for now...let's just get it over with.'

CHAPTER TWO

Where was she taking him?

Maybe he should have paid attention, but he'd stalked back into his office and worked until she'd decreed it was time to go. Then he'd walked beside her to the station and stayed silent as she organised tickets. He'd been too angry to do anything else, and too caught up in work. The Berswood faxes had come through just as he left, and he'd spotted a loophole that would have his lawyers busy for weeks.

Had they really thought he wouldn't notice such a problem?

As he walked to the station he was planning his course of attack—and maybe that was no accident. Burying himself in work had always been his way to block out the world, and he was not looking forward to the next three days. Three days immersed in his work, with little to alleviate it, with no hotel gym to burn energy… And missing Elinor and the kids… That hurt.

At least he had the Berswood contract to work on, he told himself as he strode beside his PA, trying to think the legal implications through as she purchased tickets and hurried to the train. Then as the train pulled out, the announcement came through that the train destination was four hours away. What the…?

He and Meg had been forced to sit across the aisle from each other. He looked across at her in alarm. 'Four hours?'

'We get off earlier,' she called. 'Two and a half hours.'

Two and a half hours?

He couldn't even grill her. He sat hard against the window with barely enough room to balance his laptop. Beside him, a woman was juggling two small children, one on her knee and one in a carrycot in the aisle. Meg had someone else's child on her lap. There were people squashed every which way, in a train taking them who knew where?

He was heading into the unknown, with his PA.

She didn't even look like his PA, he thought as the interminable train journey proceeded, and even the Berswood deal wasn't enough to hold his attention. It seemed she'd brought her luggage to the office so she could make a quick getaway. Once he'd grudgingly accepted her invitation, she'd slipped into the Ladies and emerged...different.

His PA normally wore a neat black suit, crisp white blouse and sensible black shoes with solid heels. She wore her hair pulled tightly into an elegant chignon. He'd never seen her with a hair out of place.

She was now wearing hip-hugging jeans, pale blue canvas sneakers—a little bit worn—and a soft white shirt, open necked, with a collar but no sleeves.

What was more amazing was that she'd tugged her chignon free, and her bouncing chestnut curls were flowing over her shoulders. And at her throat was a tiny Christmas angel.

The angel could have been under her corporate shirt for weeks, he thought, stunned at the transformation. She looked casual. She looked completely unbusinesslike—and he didn't like it. He didn't like being on this train. He didn't like it that his PA was chatting happily to the woman beside her about who knew what?

He wasn't in control, and to say he wasn't accustomed to the sensation was an understatement.

William McMaster had been born in control. His parents were distant, to say the least, and he'd learned early that nursery staff came and went. If he made a fuss, they went. He seldom did make a fuss. He liked continuity; he liked his world running smoothly.

His PA was paid to make sure it did.

Meg had come to him with impeccable references. She'd graduated with an excellent commerce degree, she'd moved up the corporate ladder in the banking sector and it was only when her personal circumstances changed that she'd applied for the job with him.

'I need to spend more time with my family,' she'd said and he hadn't asked more.

Her private life wasn't his business.

Only now it was his business. He should have asked more questions. He was trapped with her family, whoever her family turned out to be.

While back in New York…

He needed to contact Elinor, urgently, but he couldn't call her now. It was three in the morning her time. It'd have to wait.

The thought of contacting her made him feel ill. To give such disappointment…

'There's less than an hour to go,' Meg called across the aisle and, to his astonishment, she sounded cheerful. 'Dandle a baby if you're bored. I'm sure the lady beside you would be grateful.'

'I couldn't let him do that.' The young mother beside him looked shocked. 'I'd spoil his lovely suit.'

He winced. He'd taken off his jacket but he still looked corporate and he knew it. He had suits and gym gear. Nothing else.

Surely that couldn't be a problem. But…

Where were they going?

He'd had visions of a suburban house with a comfortable spare room where he could lock himself in and work for three days. He'd pay, so he wouldn't have to be social; something he'd be forced to be if he stayed with any of Melbourne's social set. But now… Where was she taking him?

He was a billionaire. He did not have problems like this.

How did you get off a train?

There was a no alcohol policy on the train, which was just as well as the carriage was starting to look like a party. It was full of commuters going home for Christmas, holidaymakers, everyone escaping the city and heading bush.

Someone started a Christmas singalong, which was ridiculous, but somehow Meg found herself singing along too.

Was she punch-drunk?

No. She was someone who'd lost the plot but there was nothing she could do about it. She had no illusions about her job. She'd messed things up and, even though she was doing the best she could, William McMaster had been denied his Christmas and she was responsible.

Worse, she was taking him home. He hadn't asked where home was. He wasn't interested.

She glanced across the aisle at him and thought he so didn't belong on this train. He looked…

Fabulous, she admitted to herself, and there it was, the thing she'd carefully suppressed since she'd taken this job. W S McMaster was awesome. He was brilliant and powerful and more. He worked her hard but he paid magnificently; he expected the best from her and he got it.

And he was so-o-o sexy. If she wasn't careful, she knew she stood every chance of having a major crush on the guy. But she'd realised that from the start, from that first interview, so she'd carefully compartmentalised her life. He was her boss. Any other sensation had to be carefully put aside.

And she'd learned from him. W S McMaster had compartments down to a fine art. There was never any hint of personal interaction between employer and employee.

But now there needed to be personal interaction. W S McMaster was coming home to her family.

He'd better be nice to Scotty.

He didn't have to be nice to anyone.

Yes, he did, she thought. For the next few days her boundaries needed to shift. Not to be taken away, she reminded herself hastily. Just moved a little. She needed to stop thinking about him as her boss and start thinking about him as someone who should be grateful to her for providing emergency accommodation.

She'd made a start, deliberately getting rid of her corporate gear, making a statement that this weekend wasn't entirely an extension of their work relationship.

He could lock himself in his room for the duration, she thought. She'd sent a flurry of texts to Letty on the subject of which room they'd put him in. The attic was best. There was a good bed and a desk and a comfy chair. It had its own small bathroom. The man was a serious workaholic. Maybe he'd even take his meals in his room.

'He's not singing,' the elderly woman beside her said. Meg had struck up an intermittent conversation with her, so she knew the connection. 'Your boss. Is he not happy?'

'He's stuck in Australia because of the airline strike,' Meg said. 'I suspect he's homesick.'

Homesick. She'd spoken loudly because of the singing, but there was a sudden lull between verses and somehow her words hit silence. Suddenly everyone was looking at William.

'Homesick,' the woman beside Meg breathed, loud enough

for everyone to hear; loud enough to catch William's attention. 'Oh, that's awful. Do you have a wife and kiddies back home?'

'I...no,' William said, clearly astonished that a stranger could be so familiar.

'So it'll just be your parents missing you,' the woman said. 'Oh, I couldn't bear it. Where's home?'

'New York.' The two syllables were said with bluntness bordering on rudeness, but the woman wasn't to be deflected.

'New York City?' she breathed. 'Oh, where? Near Central Park?'

'My apartment overlooks Central Park,' he conceded, and there was an awed hush.

'Will it be snowing there?' someone asked, and Meg looked at her boss's grim face and answered for him. She'd checked the forecast. It was part of her job.

'The forecast is for snow.'

'Oh, and the temperature here's going to be boiling.' The woman doing the questioning looked as if she might burst into tears on his behalf. 'You could have made snowmen in Central Park.'

'I don't...'

'Or thrown snowballs,' someone added.

'Or made a Snowman Santa.'

'Hey, did you see that movie where they fell down and made snow angels?'

'He could do that here in the dust.'

There was general laughter, but it was sympathetic, and then the next carol started and William was mercifully left alone.

Um...maybe she should have protected him from that. Maybe she shouldn't have told anyone he was her boss. Meg looked across at William—immersed in his work again— and thought—I'm taking my boss home for Christmas and all we're offering is dust angels. He could be having a white Christmas in Central Park.

With who?

She didn't know, and she was not going to feel bad about that, she decided. Not until he told her that he was missing a person in particular. If he was simply going to sit in a luxury penthouse and have lobster and caviar and truffles and open gifts to himself...

She was going home to Scotty and Grandma and a hundred cows.

That was a good thought. No matter how appallingly she'd messed up, she was still going home for Christmas.

She was very noble to share, she told herself.

Hold that thought.

Tandaroit wasn't so much a station as a rail head. There'd been talk of closing it down but Letty had immediately presented a petition with over five thousand names on it to their local parliamentarian. No matter that Letty, Scotty and Meg seemed to be the only ones who used it—and that the names on the petition had been garnered by Letty, dressed in gumboots and overalls, sitting on the corner of one of Melbourne's major pedestrian malls in Scotty's now discarded wheelchair. She'd been holding an enormous photograph of a huge-eyed calf with a logo saying 'Save Your Country Cousins' superimposed.

Tandaroit Station stayed.

When Letty wanted something she generally got it. Her energy was legendary. The death of her son and daughter-in-law four years ago had left her shattered, but afterwards she'd hugged Meg and she'd said, 'There's nothing to do but keep going, so we keep going. Let's get you another job.'

Meg's first thought had been to get some sort of accountancy job in Curalo, their closest city, but then they'd found Mr McMaster's advertisement. 'You'd be away from us almost completely for three months of the year but the rest we'd have you almost full-time. That'd be better for Scotty; better for all of us. And look at the pay,' Letty had said, awed. 'Oh, Meg, go for it.'

So she'd gone for it, and now she was tugging her bag down from the luggage rack as William extricated himself from his wedged in position and she was thinking that was what she had to do now. Just go for it. Christmas, here we come, ready or not.

Her bag was stuck under a load of other people's baggage. She gave it a fierce tug and it came loose, just as William freed himself from his seat. She lurched backward and he caught her. And held.

He had to hold her. The train was slowing. There were youngsters sitting in the aisle, she had no hope of steadying herself and she had every chance of landing on top of a child. But her boss was holding her against him, steady as a rock in the swaying train.

And she let him hold her. She was tired and unnerved and overwrought. She'd been trying to be chirpy; trying to pretend everything was cool and she brought someone like her boss home for Christmas every year. She'd been trying to think that she didn't care that she'd just ruined the most fantastic job she'd ever be likely to have.

And suddenly it was all just too much. For one fleeting moment she let her guard down. She let herself lean into him, while she felt his strength, the feel of his new-this-morning crisp linen shirt, the scent of his half-a-month's-salary aftershave…

'Ooh, I hope you two have a very happy Christmas,' the lady she'd been sitting near said, beaming up at them in approval. 'No need for gifts for you two, then. No wonder you're taking him home for Christmas.' And then she giggled. 'You know, I married my boss too. Best thing I ever did. Fourteen grandchildren later... You go for it, love.'

And Meg, who'd never blushed in her life, turned bright crimson and hauled herself out of her boss's arms as if she were burned.

The train was shuddering to a halt. She had to manoeuvre her way through the crowds to get out.

She headed for the door, leaving her boss to follow. If he could. And she wouldn't really mind if he couldn't.

The train dumped them and left, rolling away into the night, civilisation on wheels, leaving them where civilisation wasn't. Nine o'clock on the Tandaroit rail head. Social hub of the world. Or not. There was a single electric light above the entrance, and nothing else for as far as the eye could see.

'So...where exactly are we?' William said, sounding as if he might have just landed on Mars, but Meg wasn't listening. She was too busy staring out into the night, willing the headlights of Letty's station wagon to appear.

Letty was always late. She'd threatened her with death if she was late tonight.

She couldn't even phone her to find out where she was. There was no mobile reception out here. And, as if in echo of her thoughts...

'There's no reception.' Her boss was staring incredulously at his phone.

'There's a land line at the farm.'

'You've brought me somewhere with no cellphone reception?'

Hysterics were once again very close to the surface. Meg felt ill. 'It's better than sleeping at the airport,' she snapped, feeling desperate.

'How is it better?' He was looking where she was looking, obviously hoping for any small sign of civilisation. There wasn't any. Just a vast starlit sky and nothing and nothing and nothing.

'She'll come.'

'Who'll come?'

'My grandmother,' Meg said through gritted teeth. 'If she knows what's good for her, she'll come right now.'

'Your home is how far from the station?'

'Eight miles.'

'Eight!'

'Maybe a bit more.'

'It's a farm?'

'Yes.'

'So Tandaroit…'

She took a couple of deep breaths. Hysterics would help no one. 'It's more of a district than a town,' she admitted. 'There was a school here once, and tennis courts. Not now, though. They use the school for storing stock feed.'

'And your farm's eight miles from this…hub,' he said, his voice carefully, dangerously neutral. 'That's a little far to walk.'

'We're not walking.'

'I was thinking,' he said, 'of how long it might take to walk back here when I decide to leave.'

That caught her. She stopped staring out into the night and stared at her boss instead. Thinking how this might look to him.

'You mean if my family turn into axe-murderers?' she ventured.

'I've seen *Deliverance*.'

Her lips twitched. 'We're not that bad.'

'You don't own a car?'

'No.'

'Yet I pay you a very good wage.'

'We have Letty's station wagon and a tractor. What else do we need?'

'You like sitting on rail heads waiting for grandmothers who may or may not appear?'

'She'll appear.'

'I believe,' he said, speaking slowly, as if she was ever so slightly dim, 'that I might be changing my mind about travelling to a place that's eight miles from a train which comes... how often a day?'

'Three or four times, but it only stops here once.'

'Once,' he said faintly. 'It stops once, eight miles away from a place that has no mobile phone reception, with a grandmother who even her granddaughter appears to be feeling homicidal about.'

Uh-oh. She ran her fingers through her hair and tried to regroup.

'Not that it's not a very kind invitation,' he added and she choked. She was so close to the edge...

'I thought it was kind,' she managed.

'Kind?'

'I could have left you in the office.'

'Or not. It was you,' he reminded her, 'who got me into this mess.'

'You could have listened to the news on the radio this morning as well as me,' she snapped and then thought—had she really said that? What little hope she had of keeping her job had finally gone.

'That's what I pay you for,' he snapped back.

Well, if she'd gone this far... 'I left the office at eleven last night. I was at your hotel just after six. I don't get eight hours off?'

'I pay you for twenty-four hours on call.'

'I'm not fussed about what you pay me,' she snapped. The tension of the last few hours was suddenly erupting, and there was no way she could keep a lid on her emotions. 'I'm fussed about the ten minutes I spent washing my hair this morning when I should have been listening to the radio and hearing about the airline strike. I'm fussed about being stuck with my boss, who doesn't seem the least bit grateful that I'm doing the best I can. And now I'm stuck with someone who has the capacity to mess with my family Christmas if he doesn't stop making me feel guilty and if he spends the rest of Christmas playing Manhattan Millionaire stuck here, and it's All My Fault.'

She stopped. Out of breath. Out of emotion. Out of words. And it seemed he was the same.

Well, what could he say? Should he agree? He could hardly sack her here, right now, Meg thought. If he did...she and Letty really could be axe-murderers.

Or they could just leave him here, sitting on the Tandaroit station until the next train came through late tomorrow.

'Don't do it,' he growled, and she remembered too late he had an uncanny ability to read her mind. He hesitated and then obviously decided he had no choice but to be a little bit conciliatory. 'It's very...clean hair,' he ventured.

'Thank you.' What else was there to say?

'This...grandmother...'

'Letty.'

'She's backed up by other family members? With other cars?' He was obviously moving on from her outburst, deciding the wisest thing was to ignore it.

'Just Letty.'

'And...who else?'

'Scotty. My kid brother.'

'You said no children,' he said, alarmed.

'Fifteen's not a child.'

'Okay,' he conceded. 'Who else?'

'No one.'

'Where are your parents?'

'They died,' she said. 'Four years ago. Car crash.'

He was quick. He had it sorted straight away. 'Which is why you took the job with me?'

'So I could get home more,' she said. 'Ironic, isn't it?'

But he was no longer listening. Had he been listening, anyway? 'Could this be Letty?' he demanded.

Oh, please... She stared into the darkness, and there it was, two pinpricks of light in the distance, growing bigger.

Headlights.

'*Deliverance*,' she muttered and her boss almost visibly flinched.

'Just joking,' she said.

'Don't joke.'

'No jokes,' she agreed and took a deep breath and picked up her holdall. 'Okay, here's Letty and, while you may not appreciate it, we really are safe. We've organised you a nice private bedroom with Internet. You can use our telephone if there are people you need to contact other than over the Web. You can stay in your room and work all Christmas but Letty is one of the world's best cooks and here really is better than camping in the office.'

'I imagine it will be,' he said, but he didn't sound sure. 'And I am grateful.'

'I bet you are.'

'It's lovely hair,' he said, surprisingly. 'It would have been a shame to leave it dirty for Christmas.'

'Thank you,' she managed again. Cheering up, despite herself.

Letty was coming. She could send W S McMaster to his allocated room and she could get on with Christmas.

Anger was counterproductive. Anger would get him nowhere.

Yes, his PA had messed up his Christmas plans but the

thing was done. And no, he should never have agreed to come with her to this middle-of-nowhere place. If he'd thought it through, maybe he could have rung a realtor and even bought a small house. Anything rather than being stuck at the beck and call of one wiry little woman called Letty who seemed to own the only set of wheels in the entire district.

They hadn't passed another car. The car they were in sounded sick enough to be worrying. There was something wrong with its silencer—as if it didn't have one. The engine was periodically missing. The gearbox seemed seriously shot. They were jolting along an unsealed road. He was wedged in the back seat with both his and Meg's gear and Letty was talking at the top of her lungs.

'I'm late because Dave Barring popped over to check on Millicent. Millicent's a heifer I'm worried is going to calve over Christmas.' Letty was yelling at him over her shoulder. 'Dave's our local vet and he's off for Christmas so I wanted a bit of reassurance. He reckons she should be right,' she told Meg. 'Then I had to pick up three bags of fertiliser from Robertson's. Robby said if I didn't take it tonight the place'd be locked up till after New Year. So I'm sorry it's a bit squashed in the back.'

'I'm fine,' he said. He wasn't.

Anger was counterproductive. If he said it often enough he might believe it.

'We can swap if you want,' Meg said.

'You won't fit in the back,' Letty said. 'Not with Killer.'

Letty was right. The combination of Meg and Killer would never fit in the back seat with the baggage.

Killer looked like a cross between a Labrador and an Old English sheepdog. He was huge and hairy and black as the night around them. He'd met Meg with such exuberance that once more William had had to steady her, stopping her from being pushed right over.

While Killer had greeted Meg, Letty had greeted him with a handshake that was stronger than a man's twice her size. Then she'd greeted her granddaughter with a hug that made Meg wince, and then she'd moved into organisational mode.

'You in the back. Meg, in the front with Killer. I told Scotty I'd be back by nine-thirty so we need to move.'

They were moving. They were flying over the corrugated road with a speed that made him feel as if he was about to lose teeth.

'So what do we call you?' Letty said over her shoulder.

'I told you; he's Mr McMaster,' Meg said, sounding muffled, as well she might under so much dog.

'Mac?' Letty demanded.

'He's my boss,' Letty said, sounding desperate. 'He's not Mac.'

'He's our guest for Christmas. What do we call you?' she demanded again. 'How about Mac?'

Do not let the servants become familiar.

Master William.

Mr McMaster.

Sir.

Once upon a time a woman called Hannah had called him William. To her appalling cost…

'How about Bill?' Letty demanded. 'That's short for William. Or Billy.'

'Billy?' Meg said, sounding revolted. 'Grandma, can we…'

'William,' he said flatly, hating it.

'Willie?' Letty said, hopeful.

'William.'

Letty sighed. 'Will's better. Though it is a bit short.'

'Like Meg,' Meg said.

'You know I like Meggie.'

'And you know I don't answer to it. We don't have to call you anything you don't like,' Meg said over her shoulder. 'I'm happy to keep calling you Mr McMaster.'

'You are not,' Letty retorted. 'Not over Christmas. And why are you calling him Mr McMaster, anyway? How long have you worked for him? Three years?'

'He calls me Miss Jardine.'

'Then the pair of you need to come off your high horses,' Letty retorted. 'Meg and William it is, and if I hear any sign of Ms or Mr then it's Meggie and Willie for the rest of Christmas. Right?'

'Okay with me,' Meg said, resigned.

'Fine,' William said.

Define *fine*.

He was expecting hillbilly country. What he got was *Fantasia*. They sped over a crest and there it was, spread out before them, a house straight out of a fairy tale.

Or not. As he got closer…

Not a fairy tale. A Christmas tableau.

The farmhouse, set well back from the road among scattered gums, was lit up like a series of flashing neon signs. It was so bright it should almost be visible from the next state.

'Oh, my…' Meg breathed before William could even get his breath back. 'Grandma, what have you done?'

'We both did it,' Letty said proudly. 'Me and Scotty. You like our sleigh?'

The house had two chimneys, with what looked like an attic between them. The sleigh took up the entire distance between chimneys. There was a Santa protruding from the chimney on the left. Or, rather, part of Santa. His lower half. His legs were waving backwards and forwards, as if Santa had become stuck in descent. The movement wasn't smooth, so he moved gracefully from left to right, then jerked back with a movement sharp enough to dislodge vertebrae.

The house was Christmas City. There were lights from one end to the other, a myriad of fairy lights that made the house look like something out of a cartoon movie.

'It took us days,' Letty said, pleased with the awed hush. 'When you rang and said there was a chance you couldn't get home tonight Scotty and I were ready to shoot ourselves. We've worked our tails off getting this right.'

'I can see that you have,' Meg said, sounding as stunned as he was. 'Grandma…'

'And, before you say a word, we got it all over the Internet,' Letty informed her. 'Scotty found it. It was a package deal advertised in July by some lady cleaning out her garage. She'd just bought the house and found it, and she practically paid us to take it away. Some people,' she said, slowing the car so they could admire the house in all its glory, 'have no appreciation of art.'

'But running it,' Meg said helplessly. 'It'll cost…'

'It's practically all solar,' Letty cut in. 'Except Santa. Well, there's not a lot of solar Santa Claus's backsides out there. We haven't quite got the legs right, but I'll adjust them before Christmas. Still… What do you think?'

There was suddenly a touch of anxiety in her voice. William got it, and he thought maybe this lady wasn't as tough as she sounded. She surely wanted to please this girl, Meg, sitting somewhere under her dog.

'You climb up on that roof again and I'll give all of your Christmas presents to the dogs. But I love it,' Meg said as the car came to a halt.

'Really?'

'I really love it.' Meg giggled. 'It's kitsch and funny and those legs are just plain adorable.'

'What do you think?' Letty said, and she swivelled and looked straight at him. 'Will?'

'William. Um…'

'No lies,' she said. 'Is my Meg just humouring me?'

Meg swivelled too. She was covered in dog but somehow he managed to see her expression.

Mess with my grandma and I'll mess with you, her look said, and it was such a look that he had to revise all over again what he thought of his competent, biddable PA.

His hostess for Christmas.

'Adorable,' he said faintly.

'You're lying,' Letty said, and he found himself smiling.

'I am,' he agreed, and he met Meg's glare square on. 'There's nothing adorable about a pair of crimson trousers stuck in a chimney. However, it's fantastical and truly in the spirit of Christmas. As soon as we came over the crest I just knew this was going to be a Christmas to remember.'

'Better than being stuck in the office?' Meg said, starting to smile.

'Better than the office.' Maybe.

'Then that's okay,' Letty said, accelerating again. 'If you like my decorations then you can stay. The pair of you.'

'You're very generous,' William said.

'We are, aren't we?' Meg agreed, and hugged her dog.

And then the car pulled to a halt beside the house—and straight away there was more dog. Killer's relatives? William opened the door and four noses surged in, each desperate to reach him. They were all smaller than Killer, he thought with some relief. Black and white. Collies?

'Fred, Milo, Turps, Roger, leave the man alone,' Meg called and the dog pack headed frantically for the other side of the car to envelope someone they obviously knew and loved. Meg was on the ground hugging handfuls of ecstatic dog, being welcomed home in truly splendid style.

William extricated himself from the car and stared down at her. Any hint of his cool, composed PA had disappeared. Meg was being licked from every angle, she was coated with dog and she was showing every sign of loving it.

'Killer's Meg's dog,' Letty said, surveying the scene in satisfaction. 'Fred and Roger are mine. Turps and Milo belong to Scotty but they all love Meg. She's so good with dogs.'

Meg was well and truly buried—and the sight gave him pause.

In twenty-four hours he should be entering his apartment overlooking Central Park. His housekeeper would have come in before him, made sure the heating was on, filled the place with provisions, even set up a tasteful tree. The place would be warm and elegant and welcoming.

Maybe not as welcoming as this.

He would have been welcomed almost as much as this on Christmas Day, he thought, and that was a bleak thought. A really bleak thought. The disappointment he'd felt when he'd learned of the air strike hit home with a vengeance.

He didn't show emotion. He was schooled not to show it. But now...

It wasn't any use thinking of it, he thought, struggling to get a grip on his feelings. Elinor would make alternative arrangements. The kids were accustomed to disappointment.

That made it worse, not better.

Don't think about it. Why rail against something he could do nothing about?

Why was the sight of this woman rolling with dog intensifying the emotion? Making him feel as if he was on the outside looking in?

Back off, he told himself. He was stuck here for three days. Make the most of it and move on.

Meg was struggling to her feet and, despite a ridiculous urge to go fend off a few dogs, he let her do it herself, regain her feet and her composure, or as much composure as a woman who'd just been buried with dogs could have.

'No, down. Oh, I've missed you guys. But where's Scotty?'

Scotty was watching them.

The kid in the doorway was tall and gangly and way too skinny, even allowing for an adolescent growth spurt. He had Meg's chestnut curls, Meg's freckles, Meg's clear green eyes, but William's initial overriding impression was that he looked almost emaciated. There was a scar running the length of his left cheek. He had a brace enclosing his left leg, from foot to hip.

He was looking nervously at William, but as soon as William glanced at him he turned his attention to his sister. Who'd turned her attention to him.

'Scotty...' Dogs forgotten, Meg headed for her brother and enveloped him in a hug that was almost enough to take him from his feet. The kid was four or five inches taller than Meg's meagre five feet four or so, but he had no body weight to hold him down. Meg could hug as much as she wanted. There was no way Scotty could defend himself.

Not that he was defending himself. He was hugging Meg back, but with a wary glance at William over her head. Suspicious.

'Hi,' William said. 'I'm William.' There. He'd said it as if it didn't hurt at all.

'I'm Scott,' the boy said, and Meg released him and turned to face William, her arm staying round her brother, her face a mixture of defensiveness and pride.

'This is my family,' she said. 'Letty and Scotty and our dogs.'

'Scott,' Scott said again, only it didn't come out as it should. He was just at that age, William thought, adolescent trying desperately to be a man but his body wasn't cooperating. His voice was almost broken, but not quite.

And, aside from his breaking voice, his leg looked a mess as well. You didn't get to wear a brace that looked like scaffolding if the bones underneath weren't deeply problematic.

Meg had told him her parents had died four years ago. Had Scott been in the same car crash? The brace spoke of serious ongoing concerns.

Why hadn't he found this out? William had always prided himself on hiring on instinct rather than background checks. A background check right now would be handy.

'Did the car get you here all right?' the kid asked, and William could see he was making an effort to seem older than he was. 'It needs about six parts replacing but Grandma won't let me touch it.'

'You mess with that car and we're stuck,' Letty said. 'Next milk cheque I'll get it seen to.'

'I wouldn't hurt it.'

'You're fifteen. You're hardly a mechanic.'

'Yeah, but I've read…'

'No,' Letty snapped. 'The car's fine.'

'I tried messing with my dad's golf cart when I was fifteen,' William said, interrupting what he suspected to be a long running battle. 'Dad was away for a month. He came back and I'd supplied him with a hundred or so extra horsepower. Sadly, he touched the accelerator and hit the garage door. The fuss! Talk about lack of appreciation.'

Scott smiled at that—a shy smile but a smile nonetheless. So did Letty, and so did Meg. And his reaction surprised him.

He kind of liked these smiles, he decided. They took away a little of the sting of the last few hours. It seemed he could put thoughts of *Deliverance* aside. These people were decent. He could settle down here and get some work done.

And maybe he could try and make Meg smile again. Was that a thought worth considering?

'The Internet's down,' Scott said and smiling was suddenly the last thing on his mind.

'The Internet…' Meg said, sounding stunned. 'What's wrong with it?'

'There's been a landslip over at Tandaroit South and the lines are down. They don't know when it'll be fixed. Days probably.'

He was having trouble figuring this out. 'Lines?'

'Telephone lines,' Scott said, an adolescent explaining something to slightly stupid next-generation-up.

'You use phone lines for the Internet?'

'I know, dinosaur stuff and slow as,' Scott said. 'But satellite connection costs heaps. Mickey has satellite connection, but Meg's only just figured out a way we can afford dial-up.'

'And…' He checked his phone. 'There's no mobile reception here either,' he said slowly.

'No,' Meg told him.

'And now no fixed phone?'

'No.' Meg sounded really nervous—as well she might.

'So no Internet until the line's fixed?'

'Well, duh,' Scott said, sounding adolescent and a bit belligerent. Maybe he thought his sister was about to be attacked. Maybe she was.

But William wasn't focused on Meg. He was feeling ill. To be so far from contact… He should have rung Elinor before he left Melbourne. He should have woken her.

He *had* to contact her. Her entire Christmas would be ruined.

'I can't stay here,' he said through gritted teeth. 'The airport'd be better than this.'

'Hey!' Letty said.

He didn't have time or space to pacify her. All he could think of was Elinor—and two small kids. 'I need to use a phone,' he snapped. 'Now.'

'I have supper on,' Letty said.

'This is important. There are people waiting for me in New York.'

'But you're not due there until tomorrow,' Meg said, astounded. 'They'll hardly be waiting at the airport yet.'

'I still need a phone. Sort it, Jardine,' he ordered.

He watched her long thoughtful stare, the stare he'd come to rely on. This woman was seriously good. He depended on her in a crisis.

He was depending on her now, and she didn't let him down.

'Supper first,' she said at last. 'If it can wait that long.'

Maybe it could, he conceded. 'Supper first. Then what?'

'Then I'll take you over to Scotty...to Scott's friend, Mickey's. Mickey lives two miles north of here and his parents have satellite connection. You can use the Internet or their Skype phone for half an hour while I catch up with Mickey's mum. The weekend before Christmas she'll probably still be up.'

'I need it for more...'

'Half an hour max,' she said, blunt and direct, as he'd come to expect. 'Even that's a favour. They're dairy farmers and it's late now. But you should be able to talk to New York via Skype. Mind, it'll be before seven in the morning over there, so trying to wake anyone up...'

'She'll wake.'

'Of course she will,' she said, almost cordially, and he looked at her with suspicion.

'Miss Jardine...'

'I'm Meg,' she said. 'Remember? Meg until I'm back on the payroll, if that ever happens.'

'I don't believe I've fired you.'

'So you haven't,' she said. 'And Christmas miracles happen. Okay, I'll take you over to Mickey's and I will try and get you in touch with New York but let's not go anywhere until we've had some of Letty's mango trifle. You have made me mango trifle, haven't you, Grandma?'

'Of course.'

'Then what are we waiting for?' she demanded, and she grabbed her bag, manoeuvred her way through her dog pack and headed inside. 'Trifle, yay.' Then she paused. 'Oh, I'm sorry, sir,' she said, looking back. 'I mean… William. Do you want your mango trifle in your room? Do you want me to take you straight there?'

'Um…no,' he said weakly.

'That's a shame,' she said. 'If you're sitting at the kitchen table you'll want seconds. There's less for us that way, but if you're sure… Lead the way, Grandma. Let's go.'

CHAPTER THREE

AN HOUR later, fortified with a supper of huge ham sandwiches and a mango trifle which seemed to have stunned
William, they were in the car again, heading for Mickey's. It
was almost eleven but Meg knew enough of Mickey to believe
he'd still be awake, Net surfing.

This was the only option for her boss to contact home. It
had to work.

Who did he have waiting for him in New York? He wasn't
saying, and she wasn't asking. They drove in silence.

She pulled up outside a farmhouse a lot less startling than
Letty's. Instead of knocking, though, while William watched
from the car, she tossed gravel at the lit end window.

Mickey hauled up the window. 'Bruce?'

That one word deflected her thoughts from her own problems. Once upon a time, Mickey would have expected Scott,
Meg thought bleakly. The kids were the same age and they
lived barely two miles apart. Four years ago, their bikes had
practically created a rut in the road between.

But the rut had long been repaired. Tonight Scott had
been too tired to come with them. He was always tired. He'd
hardly touched his supper. His school work was slipping; he
was simply uninterested. There were problems apart from

his physical ones, she thought. In the New Year she'd have to talk to his doctors again about depression.

But how could she sort depression for a kid facing what Scott was facing? How long before he could ride a bike again? He believed he never could.

She hadn't accepted it, though. She'd fight it every inch of the way. But that meant staying employed so she could pay the bills. It also meant being nice to her boss over Christmas, or as nice as she could. Which meant throwing stones at a neighbour's window three days before Christmas.

'Bruce?' Mickey called again and she hauled her attention back to here and now. 'It's Meg,' she called to the kid at the window.

'Meg?' Mickey sounded pleased, and she liked that. She liked coming home. She liked it that every person in the tiny shopping town of Tandaroit East knew her, and she could go into every house in the district and find people she knew.

'The phones are out and I have a guest here who needs to contact New York,' she said. 'Scotty…Scott said you have Skype.'

'Hey, I do,' Mickey said, sounding inordinately pleased. 'I've never used it for New York, though. I don't know anyone there.'

'Would it be all right if Mr McMaster used it?'

'William,' said William.

'Hi, Will.' Mickey was clearly delighted to have company.

'Are your parents asleep?' Meg asked.

'Dad is. He's gotta milk at five. But Mum's making mince pies. You want me to tell her you're here?'

'Yes, please,' Meg said thankfully. 'I don't want to be caught creeping round the place at night without your parents knowing.'

'Yeah,' Mickey said in a laughing voice that said such an action had indeed been indulged in on more than one occasion before now.

And Meg thought sadly of how much of a normal kid's life Scotty was missing.

So her boss used Skype while Meg helped Mickey's mum scoop mincemeat into pastry shells. Jenny wasn't much older than Meg, but while Meg had gone to university and then to a career, Jenny had married her childhood sweetheart at seventeen and had Mickey nine months later.

She could have done the same, Meg thought, feeling nostalgic and a bit jealous as she took in the cosy farm kitchen, the muddle of Christmas baking, the detritus of a farming family, with twin girls of nine as well as Mickey.

'This place looks gorgeous,' Meg said, sitting on an ancient kitchen chair and scooping mincemeat.

'Nope,' Jenny said and grinned. 'Gorgeous is what's up in Mickey's room right now.' Jenny had been introduced before Mickey had taken William off to link him with the other side of the world, and Meg could see her friend adding two and two and making seventeen.

'You mean my boss.'

'I mean the man you've brought home for Christmas. Yum. I've seen him in the gossip rags and he's even more gorgeous in the flesh. He's a squillionaire. He's your boss. And you've got him for Christmas.'

'You can have him if you want him,' Meg said morosely. 'He might be happier here. You have a computer.'

'Yeah, and I have twins and Ian's extended family arriving tomorrow to stay for a week. There'll be eight kids in the house. Heaven help us.' But she was smiling as she said it and Meg thought, even though she had never understood Jenny's decision to marry and make a home so early, maybe… just maybe it made sense.

'You're not getting clucky,' Jenny demanded, following her gaze, and Meg realised she was staring at a pile of paper chains at the far end of the table. She remembered making them as a kid.

'I have spare paper,' Jenny said happily. 'You can help your boss make paper chains. Very bonding.'

'Very funny.'

'No, I think it's lovely,' Jenny said, getting serious. 'To have him here for Christmas… Oooh, Meg. But does he have a girlfriend?'

'I have no idea.'

'No idea?'

'Well, I'm his PA and I haven't been told to send flowers to anyone lately. But he was desperate to use the phone.'

'So who's he ringing?'

'I have no idea.'

'I'll ask Mickey.'

But Mickey, who wandered into the kitchen two minutes later, was no help at all.

'Yeah, he's talking but I put my headset on and left him to it. Nah, I didn't hear who to. Mum, you reckon it's too late to put another CD on my Christmas list? I've just found this sick new band…'

'Forget it,' his mother said. 'Santa asked for a list a month ago and you couldn't think of anything except a farm bike, which you know we can't afford. So what are you giving William for Christmas, Meg, love?'

Uh-oh. Here was yet another problem she hadn't thought through.

On Christmas morning she sat under the Christmas tree and opened presents. Lots of presents.

Meg's mother had always believed in…excess. She'd loved

Christmas with a passion and Meg had still been getting a Santa stocking at twenty-five.

The next year, with her parents dead, Meg had over-compensated, and so had Letty and, to their delight, so did Scott. He'd plundered his piggy bank and asked the nurses to help him.

They'd had a silly, over-the-top Christmas in Scotty's hospital ward, and the tradition had thus continued.

So Meg's last minute Christmas spree had filled her baggage with gifts but there wasn't a lot she could recycle for William.

'He has everything,' she said, feeling hopeless.

'He hasn't got Skype,' Mickey said.

'He will next week when he goes back to New York.'

'So buy him a satellite dish for the weekend,' Mickey said cheerfully. 'Then Scotty can use it after he leaves.'

Right. With what?

'That's just a bit more money than I had in mind to spend,' she retorted and Mickey screwed up his nose and sloped off to watch television in the other room. Grown-up problems. Not his.

'So how's the debt reduction going?' Jenny asked. Jenny had been one of the many who'd come to Meg's aid after the crash. She knew of Meg's debt. Scott's medical expenses were colossal, and on top of that they'd had to keep the farm going when there was no one to run it.

'It's okay,' she told her friend. As long as I'm not sacked, she added under her breath. But I'm probably sacked, so let's not go there.

'So it's just a present for Mr Sexy-Eyes. Can you knit?'

'No!'

'So that's home-made socks out of the question. Leaves only aftershave,' Jenny said. 'Ian gets some every year from his Aunty Merle, only Merle hasn't noticed that Ian's had a full beard for twenty years now. I'm happy to donate a gallon or six.'

'I suspect he uses his own.'

'I guess he would,' Jenny said, sliding one batch of mince pies out of the oven and another in. 'So there's nothing in the world he needs.'

'Except a plane out of here.'

'Out of your control, love,' Jenny said. 'It'll have to be aftershave.' She glanced up at the ceiling. 'I'd so love to be a fly on the wall, wouldn't you? I wonder who he's talking to?'

'It's not my business,' Meg said, a bit too primly, and Jenny laughed.

'You mean the walls are too thick and there's no way we can find out. Let's face it, you're interested, and why not? He's the most eligible man on the planet, as well as the most gorgeous. As well as that, he's your house guest for three days. You have him trapped. Meg darling, if you don't try and get him interested—seriously interested—you have rocks in your head.'

'Finished,' William's voice growled from the door and they both jumped and Meg did her blushing thing again. That was twice now. All I want for Christmas is my dignity, she thought desperately, as Jenny stifled laughter.

'Did…did you get onto who you wanted?' she managed, wondering how pink her face was.

'Yes, thank you.' How much had he heard? she thought. *The most eligible man on the planet…* And… *You have him trapped…* If he thought…

'Who did you need to talk to?' Jenny asked innocently and offered him a plate of mince pies.

'Friends,' he said shortly, his face expressionless. Meg knew that expression. It meant the McMaster displeasure was about to wreak consequences. There wasn't a lot of wreaking he could do right now, though, except wave away the mince pie plate as if it was poison.

'Eat my mince pies or I'll be offended for ever,' Jenny said. 'The price of my Internet café is a compliment for the cook.'

And he really was trapped, Meg thought. He was forced not to snap; he was forced even to be pleasant.

So he ate and he somehow managed to tell Jenny her mince pies were excellent, while Meg tried to get her face in order, and she almost managed it but then Jenny, dog at a bone, refusing to be deflected, said, 'So are you going to tell us who this friend is who's awake at six o'clock in the morning in New York?' and Meg blushed all over again.

'Jenny, he doesn't have to answer.'

'No, but I'm interested.'

'Thank you very much for your Internet use,' William said, clipped, tight and angry. He tugged his wallet out and laid a note on the kitchen table. A note so large it made Jenny gasp.

'What do you think you're doing?'

'Paying,' he said.

'Put it away,' Jenny said, angry to match now. 'There's no need for that.'

'Jenny's my friend,' Meg said. 'She'd never charge.'

'She's not *my* friend.'

Whoa. Line overstepped. She was home for Christmas and there were some things which she would not put up with. Hurting Jenny was one of them.

'She is because she let you use the Internet when she didn't have to. Without thought of payment. You won't have to walk back to the station. I'll drive you,' she snapped. 'Jenny, do you have a sleeping bag I can borrow? And a water bottle? Give him a couple more of those mince pies so he won't starve.'

'Hey, I wasn't that offended,' Jenny said, her flash of hurt disappearing and being replaced by her customary laughter. She took William's money and tucked it back into his suit pocket. 'It was very nice of him to offer.'

'It was not nice,' Meg said, glowering. 'He was being snarky.'

'Snarky?' William said.

'Don't look at me like I'm speaking some other language,' Meg retorted. 'You know what snarky is. Jenny. Sleeping bag.'

'You're not serious,' Jenny said. 'If you are, he can sleep here.'

'He's not your friend. He just said so.'

'He wasn't serious.'

'I was,' William said. 'But I'm having second thoughts.'

'You know, I think that's wise,' Jenny said, and grinned again and waggled her finger at the pair of them. 'Birds in their little nest agree...'

'Jenny!'

'Go on, get out of here, the two of you,' Jenny said cheerfully. 'Take him home, Meg, and don't even think of going via the station. Can you just see the headlines? Tomorrow's express train thundering through Tandaroit Station, with William McMaster sleeping off the effect of too many mince pies on a deserted platform? So be nice to her, William, and if you can possibly manage it, tell her who it is that you contacted tonight. She's dying to know, even if it isn't her business.'

She raised floury hands and shooed them out into the hall, out of the front door. She banged it shut after them, and then tugged it open again. An afterthought had just occurred.

'It's the season for peace on earth and goodwill to all men,' she called after them. 'So don't leave him on the railway station.'

* * *

They drove home in silence. Meg was too embarrassed to say anything. William simply…didn't.

She pulled up outside the house and made to get out, but William's hand came down onto her arm, making her pause.

'I'm sorry,' he said. 'But I don't take kindly to questions.'

'That's your right. But you will be nice to my family and to my friends.'

'I will be nice to your family and to your friends,' he repeated. 'Tell me about Scott.'

'Sorry?'

'I've employed you for three years. I've never asked about your family.

'I don't take kindly to questions,' she intoned and he grimaced.

'That's your right,' he conceded. 'Of course you're not obligated to tell me.'

'As you're not obligated to tell me who you just telephoned.' She relented then, sighed and put up her hands in mock surrender. 'No. Don't tell me. It's Jenny who wanted to know that one, not me.' And how about that for a barefaced lie? she thought, but some lies were almost compulsory.

But William's question still hung, unanswered, and he wasn't taking it back.

She glanced at the house. Apart from the Christmas decorations it was all in darkness. Letty and Scott would be long asleep. Even the dogs hadn't stirred on their return. They'd be sleeping in a huge huddle at the end of Scott's bed, she knew. Turps and Roger would be on the bed itself—Scott had trained them to lie still so he could use them as a rest for his brace. The others would be on the floor, as close as they could get.

She loved Scotty so much it hurt. It hurt so much she wanted to cry. And, all at once, it was easy to answer William's question. She wanted to talk.

'Scotty's my half-brother,' she said, staring ahead into the darkness. Speaking almost to herself. 'My mum was a single mum—she had me early and she raised me the hard way, with no parental support. Then, when I was nine, she met Scott's dad. Alex was a farmer, a fair bit older than she was. Mum was selling second-hand clothes at a market and Alex had come to town to check out some new, innovative water pump. He never bought the pump but he took one look at Mum and he fell hard.'

'Love at first sight,' William said, and he sounded a bit derisive. Meg glared at him. He was on shaky ground. Derision wasn't something she was putting up with tonight.

And apparently he realised it. 'Sorry,' he said. 'Sorry, sorry. Love at first sight. It happens.'

'So it does,' she said and glared at him a bit longer until she was sure he was remembering the railway station and the water bottle and the express train thundering through, crowded with people with cameras.

'So it did,' she reiterated as he attempted to look apologetic—not a good fit for W S McMaster but it was a start. Her glare faded. 'I remember the weekend Alex invited us here. He was a great big dairy farmer, in his forties. He hardly talked. That was okay. Mum was a talker, and I remember he just kept looking at Mum like she was some sort of magic. And then I met Letty and Letty was my magic. We arrived on the Friday night and Mum and Alex couldn't take their eyes off each other all weekend, and on Sunday Letty said "call me Grandma." It was like we'd come home. We had come home. Alex took us back to Melbourne and we threw our things into the back of his truck and we headed back here and stayed. Alex married Mum a month later. I was a flower girl. Letty made me the most gorgeous dress. We were so happy, and then five years later Scotty was born and it was perfect.'

'Nothing's perfect,' William said, as if he couldn't help himself, and she shook her head in disgust.

'And there's no such thing as love at first sight? Don't mess with my fairy tales, Mr McMaster. It was love at first sight and it was perfect for sixteen whole years. Sure, the farm's not big and we struggled a bit, but Mum still did markets and everyone helped. I was good at school and we knew there was no way the farm would support Scotty and me—or even one of us—but I was really happy going to university. I missed it more when I got a full-time job, but I was still pretty happy, having this place here as my backstop. And then four years ago a truck came round a bend on the wrong side of the road and it all crumpled to nothing.'

Silence.

'I'm so sorry,' he said at last.

'Yeah,' she said grimly. 'It makes you realise that when you have the fairy tale you hang on and you appreciate it every single moment. Just like that...' She shook her head, shaking away nightmares. 'Anyway, Mum and Alex were killed instantly. Scotty was eleven. He was in the back seat. He just broke...everything. For months we thought he'd be a paraplegic, but he had so much grit. He *has* so much grit. He's fought and fought. For ages neighbours kept the farm going for us. We thought we'd have to sell but then Letty and I figured maybe we could keep it. If we use my salary to augment the income, we can just get by. It's where Scotty's happy. It's where Letty's happy.'

'And your job with me...'

'See, there's the fairy tale again,' she said and smiled, but he didn't smile back. He looked intent, as if trying to see meaning behind her words. It disconcerted her, but no matter, she had to keep going. 'I thought I'd get a job in Curalo and commute the twenty miles,' she told him, 'but then along came your advertisement and it's been fabulous. We have a lady who comes and milks for us while I'm not here. Letty's still active. We've coped.'

'So if I sack you…'

Her smile faded. 'Then…'

'Then the fairy tale ends again?'

'It's not as bad as that,' she said and tilted her chin. 'We'll manage.'

'I won't sack you.'

'I don't need sympathy.'

'I'm not offering it. We'll put this behind us as an unfortunate aberration…'

'On my part.'

'On your part,' he agreed gravely. 'It's been a sad hiccup in your normally exemplary efficiency. We'll get this weekend behind us and then go back to where we were. You're normally an extremely competent employee.'

'Gee, thanks,' she said before she could stop herself. Who was being snarky now?

'If that's sarcasm…'

'No, I'm overwhelmed,' she said. 'Honestly I am.' She had to get herself under control here. Meek, she told herself. Do meek.

'I don't give compliments that aren't deserved,' he said stiffly and she thought—what am I doing, joshing with a guy who controls my life? But there was something about this day, or this night, this time, this season—maybe even it was just that Santa was still waggling dumbly overhead—that made her refuse to treat this as normal. She wasn't going back to being Miss Jardine; not just yet.

'You know you don't have to simply "get this weekend behind us,"' she said cautiously. 'You could enjoy it.'

'I'm hardly in a position to enjoy it.'

'Because you don't have the phone or the Internet?'

'Because I'm right out of my comfort zone,' he said honestly. 'And I want to be back in New York.'

'And I want my parents back,' she retorted. 'But that doesn't stop me enjoying what I have. The here and now.'

'That's very commendable.'

'It is, isn't it,' she said evenly. 'In fact, if I'm not mistaken, my boss just commended me. He said I was normally an extremely competent employee. So while I'm ahead I might just stop.' She swung herself out of the car and waited for him to do likewise. 'I have an early start, Mr McMaster, so I need to go to bed.'

'Why do you have an early start?'

'I milk cows,' she said, heading for the back door. 'If you can't sleep and run out of work, then you're welcome to join me at dawn. Instead of a gym workout. If I were you, though, I wouldn't wear a suit.' And she walked into the house and left him to follow—if he wanted.

What choice did he have?

None at all.

CHAPTER FOUR

HE WOKE to the sound of cows. Many cows. The window of his attic bedroom was open and the not-so-gentle lowing was filling the room. The old, comfortable bed, the faded furnishings and the unaccustomed sounds were so different from his normal environment that he struggled to take it in.

But he got it soon enough. He was trapped for Christmas. On Meg's farm.

Meg…

In the pre-dawn light the name felt strange, almost dangerous. He linked his hands loosely behind his head and stared upward, trying to assimilate how he was feeling. The planked ceiling ran up to a peak. He'd be right underneath Santa's sleigh, he thought, and that seemed so unnerving he unlinked his hands and swung himself straight out of bed.

He didn't intend to lie in bed and think about Santa. About what he'd promised. About what he was missing in New York.

Nor did he intend to lie in bed and think about Meg.

Miss Jardine.

Meg, he thought. The name suited her.

So why was Letty's order to use her name unsettling?

He knew why. As an adolescent blessed with enough insight to think about emotions, he'd struggled with reasons. He'd even wondered if one of the therapists his mother used might give him answers. But finally he'd worked it out himself. This had been a lesson taught early to a child by a jealous, vindictive mother, who believed employees and friends were to be strictly differentiated.

'They'll take advantage...'

It was a savage line, said with spite, and the memory of it still had the power to make him flinch.

Unsettled, he crossed to the attic window and peered below. It was barely daybreak; the sun wasn't yet over the horizon and the farm looked grey-green, barely lit from the night before. He could see the roof of what must be the dairy, and cows clustering beyond. A couple of dogs were fussing around them, but the cows were uninterested. The cows looked as if they knew what they were about, and the dogs were simply demonstrating their role.

A role other than licking Meg.

Meg. There it was again. The word.

'They'll take advantage...'

He'd been seven. His parents had been away, for who knew how long? It never seemed to matter because the house was much more fun with them gone. It was summer. School was out and Ros, their cook, had been teaching him to make pancakes. But she'd turned her back and he'd tried to flip a pancake before it was ready. The hot batter had oozed from the spatula and onto his hand.

Hannah, his nanny, had come running. She'd held him tight, rocking him, while Ros rushed to apply salve.

'There, baby, it'll be fine, see, Ros has ice and ointment all ready. Let Hannah see.'

His parents had walked in as they'd hugged him.

Maybe he hadn't reacted fast enough. He was shocked and his hand hurt, so instead of rushing to greet them with the pleasure he'd already begun to act instead of feel, he'd simply clung harder to his Hannah.

'What is this?' his mother had demanded with deep displeasure, and he'd sobbed then, with fright as well as pain. Already he knew that voice. 'William, stop that appalling crying and get over here. You do not get close to servants.'

'They're not servants,' he'd managed. 'They're Hannah and Ros.'

His mother's eyes had narrowed at that, and he'd been sent to his room without even salve on his hand.

Who knew where Hannah and Ros were now? They'd been given notice on the spot. He needed to learn independence, his mother had decreed, and he still remembered the sneer.

His next nanny had been nice enough, but he'd learned. His new nanny was Miss Carmichael. He did not get close.

Soon after that he'd been sent to boarding school. His parents had split and from then on his holidays had been spent with his grandparents. The only care he had there was from more servants—though eventually his grandfather realised he had a head for figures. That had resulted in a tinge of interest. William was deemed the new head of the McMaster Empire.

So there he had it, he thought ruefully, his one family use. His grandfather knew he'd make a good businessman and that was the extent of his importance. It was no wonder he was emotionally screwed.

He should be able to get over it—his dysfunctional family—their fierce focus on social hierarchy and fortune—their petty squabbles and personal vindictiveness—their total lack of sense of family. But how to get over a lifetime of dysfunction? Even now, he didn't really understand what family love or life was. He'd an inkling of it through friends and associates. At times he even envied it, but to try and achieve it... No.

He'd learned not to need it. He couldn't need something he didn't understand and the last thing he wanted was to hurt another human as his extended family had hurt each other. How could he undo so many years of family malice? He couldn't.

He told no one any lies about himself. The women he dated used his social cachet as pay-off, and that was fine by him.

And the kids? Pip and Ned? He was certainly fond of them, as fond as he ever allowed himself to be. But they called him Mr McMaster and he knew that soon he'd disappear from their lives as well. That was the way things had to be. Like now. He couldn't even be there for them at Christmas. A broken promise, like so many he'd been given as a child…

A whistle split the air, so loud it hauled him out of his reverie. Maybe that was just as well. There was little to be gained by trying to change at this stage of his life, and maybe a lot to lose. He shrugged, mocking something that was part and parcel of how he faced the world—and then he tried to figure who was whistling.

Meg had said she'd be helping with the milking. Who else was down there?

There was only one way to find out.

He checked his watch. It was five-thirty.

Early, even by his standards.

Whoever was down there knew how to work.

W S McMaster could be forgotten here. She was perfectly, gloriously happy. She was home.

Meg stomped across the baked dirt and whooshed her next cow into the bail. Friesian 87 plodded forward with resigned equanimity.

'That's Topsy,' Kerrie said. 'Her milk production's gone up twelve per cent this year. You're ace, aren't you, girl?'

'I thought Letty decided we should stop naming them.'

'That was only when she had to get rid of half the herd. It broke her heart. Now your income's so good she's decided we can name them again. She started with Millicent, and now she's moving onto the whole herd.'

Uh-oh.

'It's not so stable as you might think,' she said cautiously.

Kerrie released her cow and stretched and glanced across into the vat room, where her three little girls were playing in a makeshift playpen. 'We take one day at a time,' she said. 'We all know that.'

Maybe everyone did, Meg thought as she washed teats and attached cups. Last year Kerrie's husband had maxed out their credit cards and taken off with a girl half his age, leaving Kerrie with three babies under four. Milking here was now her sole income.

Kerrie's income was thus dependent on Meg's income. On Meg's job.

William had said he wouldn't fire her. She had to believe him. But first they had to get through Christmas.

We'll put this behind us as an unfortunate aberration...

Christmas. An aberration.

That wasn't what he'd meant, but it was how it seemed.

What was he intending to do with himself for the next three days?

'Can I help?'

She didn't have to show she was startled. The cows did it for her, backing away in alarm at this unfamiliar person in the yard. The cow Kerrie was ushering in backed right out again before Kerrie could stop her, and Kerrie swore and headed after her.

'You need to move,' Meg said swiftly. 'You're scaring the cows.'

He was in his gym gear. Black and white designer stuff with crisp white designer trainers. Very neat.

The cows weren't appreciating it.

He backed into the vat room, where the playpen was set up. The oldest of the little girls cried out in alarm and he backed out of there too.

Meg found herself smiling. Her boss, in charge of his world. Or not.

'Go back to bed,' she advised. 'It's early.'

'I don't like my PA working before me. Is there something I can do?'

'Really?'

'Really.'

Goodness. 'How are you at washing udders?' she asked, stunned.

'I learned it at kindergarten,' he said promptly and she found herself chuckling. He'd woken up on the right side of the bed, then. Maybe this could work.

'If you're serious…'

'I'm serious.'

'The cows don't like gym gear.'

'You think I should go back and put on one of my suits?'

'Um…no.' She chuckled and saw a flare of surprise in his eyes. Maybe she didn't chuckle around him enough.

Maybe she didn't chuckle at all.

'Kerrie's brother helps out here occasionally when the kids are sick,' she said. 'Ron's around your size. His overalls and gumboots are in the vat room.'

'Gumboots?'

'Wellingtons,' Kerrie said, entranced.

'This is Kerrie,' Meg said. 'Kerrie, this is William.'

'Your boss?' Kerrie asked.

'Not right this minute he's not,' she said firmly. 'Now he's offering to be a worker. You want to use Ron's gear? The cows will settle once you look familiar.' She pointed to the vat room.

'There's babies in there,' William said nervously, and both women burst out laughing.

'If you're going to give me a hard time...' William said but, to Meg's amazement, he was smiling.

'Nah, you're free labour,' Meg said, smiling right back. 'Kerrie, you're responsible for keeping Mr McMaster free of all babies. Get changed and come out and we'll introduce you to Cows One to a Hundred.

'Only now they all have names,' Kerrie reminded her. 'I'll teach you.'

'Teach us both,' Meg said. 'It seems we both need to get used to names.'

By the time they finished, the sun was already spreading warmth, promising a hot day to come. Meg set William to sluicing the dairy while she did who knew what with the equipment in the vat room. Sluicing was, William found, a curiously satisfying job, controlling a hose with enough water power to drive the mess off the ramp and into the drains. It was a manly sort of hose, he decided, and he set about enjoying himself.

Kerrie collected her kids and made to leave. 'I'll see you tonight,' she called to Meg and he thought suddenly, she looks tired.

Three kids, so small... What was she doing, milking twice a day?

'Are you milking over Christmas?' he asked, and Kerrie nodded.

'Letty and I milk twice a day. When Meg's here Letty gets time off. She needs it.'

'When do you get a sleep-in?' he asked and suddenly Meg was outside again, listening.

'With three babies?' Kerrie asked, as if sleep-ins were unheard of.

'Their dad…'

'He did a runner,' Kerrie said, with feigned indifference. 'Milking for Meg's the only thing between me and bankruptcy.'

And William glanced over at Meg, caught her urgent, unspoken message and knew it was true.

'So you're milking morning and night all over Christmas.'

'I like it,' Kerrie said.

'So if I said I'd do it for you…'

Both women drew in their breath. Meg's face went still. She obviously hadn't expected this.

'If it's okay with Meg, that is,' he said and swooshed a mess of stuff from the ramp. Swooshing felt excellent.

Meg smiled. He liked it when she smiled. How come he hadn't noticed that smile way before now?

'It's fine by me,' Meg said, 'but…'

'But I can't afford it,' Kerrie said, suddenly breathless. 'I mean…it's a lovely offer but…'

'But nothing,' Meg said, suddenly rock solid, smiling at William as if he was Santa in person. 'William's offering to do it for free. I'm sure of it. I've budgeted for your pay so this is his gift to you. Let the man be magnanimous.'

'Magnanimous?' Kerrie ventured.

'Manly,' Meg said, grinning. 'This is a very manly gesture.'

'If you're sure,' Kerrie whispered, sounding awed.

'Of course he's sure,' Meg said, smiling and smiling. 'There's so much women's work to be done over Christmas, and what do the men do? They buy a bottle of perfume at the last minute, if we're lucky. Even Scotty. He's left his Christmas shopping to the last minute and I have to take him to Curalo this morning. I'll stand outside the shop while he buys me the perfume I've told him I like and then I'll drive him home and that's his manly duty done. So here's one offering to be truly useful...'

'Wow,' Kerrie said.

'Yep, get and go before I change my mind,' William said. 'Or before I turn my hose on your boss. Happy Christmas, Kerrie.' He moved his hose so the water arced in a wide semi-circle. How long since he'd done something this hands-on? There was a pile of dried dung beside the fence. He aimed his hose and the dung flew eighteen inches in the air before heading for the drain. Deeply satisfying.

'Oh, wow,' Kerrie breathed again, and she abandoned the kids and hugged Meg. Then she eyed William—with caution—anyone would regard him with caution right now—but finally emotion got the better of sense and she darted over the yard and hugged him as well. Then she flew back to her kids and bustled them into the car and away before anyone had a chance to change their mind.

'Hey, that felt good,' Meg said, heading back into the vat room and replacing the dipstick sort of thing she was holding into the slot at the side of the vat. 'Did it feel good to you?'

He sent another cowpat into the air. 'Absolutely.'

'If you knew how much that means to Kerrie...' Then she hesitated. 'Um... Sir... What are you doing with that hose?'

Sir? She'd called him sir. Of course, that was what he was. Wasn't it? But she was looking bemused so he turned his attention back to the hose. It had made a left turn and was now aimed straight into the drain behind the cow's drinking trough, forcing the contents of the drain up and in.

Uh-oh.

'I guess the drinking trough now needs to be cleaned,' Meg said. 'We'll need to empty it, scrub it, rinse it three times and then fill it up again. We don't want contamination, do we?'

'Um...no,' he said and thought maybe there were a few skills he needed to concentrate on.

The milk tanker arrived just as he finished. The driver climbed from the cab and greeted Meg with delight.

'Hey, Meggie.'

'Meggie?' William said softly.

'Just try it…Willie,' she said with a glower that made him grin, and went to meet the driver. William listened in while they caught up. Their talk was all about milk yields and fat content and bacterial levels. Meg sounded as he was accustomed to hearing her, smoothly competent, in charge of her world. But it was such a different world.

They gossiped on while he cleaned the trough and cleaned the yard surely cleaner than it had ever been cleaned before. Then the driver started emptying the vats and Meg strode over and turned his hose off. He felt bereft.

'I was just getting good,' he said sadly.

'You can do it again tonight,' she said and he started winding the hose around the reel by hand. She leaned over and grabbed the wheel and started turning. She was showing him up here.

But there was something else happening. The angel…

Her little Christmas angel was still hanging around her neck, and it was sliding down her breasts. He noticed.

She was wearing grungy old overalls, sort of mud-brown. She was wearing…what had she called them? Gumboots. Her hair was pulled back with an elastic band and she had mud smeared down the side of her face.

The top three buttons of her overalls were undone. Her angel was nestling on the soft swell of her breasts.

Lucky angel.

Why had it taken him until now to realise how beautiful she was?

'Earth to William,' she said and he blinked and grabbed the wheel and started turning it himself, so fast the hose slipped off and he had to stop and start again.

Maybe this wasn't a good idea. Maybe he had to get away. A thought…

'You need perfume?' he asked.

'No,' she said, bemused.

He didn't think so. Perfume would hardly fit with what she was doing right now. But…

'But Scott wants to buy you perfume.'

'He wants to go Christmas shopping. I promised I'd take him to Curalo. That's our closest major shopping centre— twenty miles from here.'

'But you have things to do here, right?'

'Right,' she said cautiously.

'So could I take him?'

'You,' she said, stunned, and he thought about whether he should take personal affront at the thought that she obviously thought him—and the rest of the male species—useless, and then he caught another glimpse of that angel and thought maybe not.

'Would he mind if I took him?' he asked. 'I could find an Internet place in town and do my contacting—kill two birds with one stone.'

'That'd be fantastic,' she breathed. 'Craig here says we should have signed the contract for our milk quota before Christmas. The manager's still at work, so Craig says I can get a lift back in with him. He can bring me back when he does the next farm. But then I promised Letty I'd help do the pudding. I need to check on Millicent. I need to see to the water troughs. I'm having trouble making everything fit.'

'So it's a good idea?'

'It's a fabulous idea,' she said admiringly. Her eyes were twinkling… Maybe she was manipulating him and it was such an odd experience…

People didn't manipulate him. Had she just manipulated him?

Who knew? This was one clever woman.

'Would you be confident driving Letty's car?' she said. 'I know you can drive on our side of the road.' More admiration?

'Yes, but...'

'Scotty would love to go with you. Christmas shopping with his sister, or go Christmas shopping with a guy, someone who won't make him wait outside lingerie shops? What a choice.'

'You don't!'

'He's always scared I might.' She hesitated, and the laughter died. 'I... he's had a tough time. He'd enjoy going shopping with you rather than with me.'

'His leg...'

She glanced across at Craig but Craig was bending down to pat Killer and was obviously not in too great a rush. She turned back to William and he realised he was being assessed. She held his gaze for a long moment and then gave a decisive little nod. Whatever test there'd been, it seemed he'd passed. Manipulation was past. It was time for honesty.

'Scott's been through hell and back,' she said bluntly. 'His leg was so badly smashed they had to put in a rod instead of bone. It healed but then they had to insert another rod because he grew. That got infected.' She swallowed. 'He almost died. Again. The leg still hasn't completely healed but it will and he's okay to get around. He's really good on crutches. If you could...just do what he wants. And if you can think of anything he'd like, I'd appreciate that too. I've bought him so many computer games he surely must be over them but I'm hopeless at thinking of what a teenage boy wants. He's so restricted—but he needs a manly present.'

Her frankness was working as manipulation never could. But he could do this. He even puffed his chest a little. 'So you'd like me to take your kid brother Christmas shopping for manly presents? I can do that.'

'Ooh, you're not my boss, you're my hero,' she said and before, he could begin to guess what she intended, she stood on tiptoe and kissed him. It was a feather kiss, almost a mockery, but not quite. It was a kiss of laughter and of sudden friendship, and why it had the capacity to make him feel...

How did it make him feel?

He didn't know and it was too late to find out. Craig was replacing his hoses and yelling, 'Are you coming or not?'

'I'm coming,' she called. 'I'll just go lose my overalls and check with Scott. But this is a great idea. My milking's sorted, my brother will be happy and I have a superhero in the dairy. What more could a girl want?'

It took Meg an hour to get to the factory and back, by which time William and Scott had been gone for an hour as well. Which left Meg back at home, with no way of knowing when they'd get back.

She was worrying about her brother. She was also worrying about why she'd kissed her boss. It had been an impulsive gesture, the sort she'd make to anyone who'd done her a big favour, but somehow...it seemed more.

She couldn't think of kissing her boss. That made her feel weird. She went back to worrying about Scott.

'You're worrying he's taken him back to New York?' Letty demanded as she caught Meg looking out of the window for maybe the twentieth time.

'He can't. There are no planes.'

'You've worked for the man for three years. Don't you trust him?'

'Of course I do.'

'Then why worry? Two hours is hardly time to Christmas shop.' But then she hesitated. 'Oh, but wait. These are guys.

Half an hour there, half an hour back, five minutes at the perfume counter—yep, they should be back by now.' She grinned. 'But maybe they're doing some bonding. He misses his father, does Scotty. Pass the raisins.'

'You want me to mix the ingredients?'

'I handed you the bowl five minutes ago—so you could look at it?'

Whoops. 'Sorry.' She applied herself to her creaming. 'Why didn't you do this before?' she asked. 'Aren't puddings supposed to have been made a month ago?'

'You didn't get any time off and I was milking. I'm not getting any younger. But, back to your young man…'

'My *boss*.'

'He doesn't seem to mind hard work.'

'You say that like it's a compliment. He's addicted to work.'

'Plus he's really cute,' Letty said and eyed Meg sideways.

'He's my boss. I hadn't noticed.'

'Right,' Letty said dryly.

Right?

So, okay she had noticed. What normal warm-blooded woman wouldn't notice W S McMaster?

But what use was there in noticing? For the three years she'd worked for him their relationship had been totally businesslike. Her boss worked far too hard for it to be anything else. He never noticed *her*, she thought. She was just one of his four PAs.

But sometimes… Sometimes when they'd been on a trip together, when they'd been working late, when she'd suddenly been a little too close, maybe even a little too familiar as tiredness crept in at the edges, she'd thought he made a conscious decision not to notice her, as if there were some barrier he couldn't cross.

As, of course, there was. He was her employer.

He was a billionaire.

She mixed the ingredients with her hands, letting the warmth of her hands meld the mixture. She was still staring out of the kitchen window, but she was no longer looking for the absent Scott and William. She was thinking of William as he'd been this morning. Mucking round with his hose. Enjoying himself.

She'd kissed him.

It had been nothing but a silly gesture, she told herself. It meant nothing.

Only that wasn't quite true. Meg Jardine had kissed William McMaster. The lines between boss and secretary had blurred.

Leading where?

'You think that might be creamed enough?' Letty demanded and she looked down into the bowl and thought yep, it was getting so warm it was starting to melt.

There was an analogy somewhere here. Melting...

'You want me to chop some nuts?' she managed and Letty grinned some more and handed them over.

'Go right ahead. A girl's gotta vent her spleen on something. You're wondering how much perfume those boys are intending to buy, or are you wondering something else entirely?'

CHAPTER FIVE

THEY didn't appear for lunch and an hour later Meg was really starting to worry. 'I'll take the tractor over to Jenny's and phone him from there,' she muttered. 'They should be back.'

'You'll do no such thing,' Letty told her. 'They'll have found a football game or gone to the movies or chanced on something really interesting that only boys can understand. You didn't tell them a get-home-by time, for which I'm grateful because it's time we stopped mollycoddling our Scotty. Our Scott.' Then she spoiled it by glancing at the clock. 'But I hope Will's fed him. And he didn't take any painkillers. If his leg's hurting…'

'See,' Meg retorted and they both smiled, shamefaced.

'Shortbread next,' Letty declared, so they made a batch, and then another, and they were almost desperate enough to start a third when finally the car turned into the drive. Meg just happened to be looking out of the window when it did.

'What on earth have they got on behind?' she demanded, heading for the door.

The dogs were flying down from the veranda. Meg managed to stroll out with what she hoped was a little more dignity.

'Don't say we were worried,' Letty hissed beside her and she agreed entirely. They hadn't been worried at all.

What did they have behind the car?

A trailer. A really large trailer. And on the trailer...

'They've bought a car,' she muttered in amazement. Or... two cars?

'So much for perfume,' Letty muttered. 'This is never going to fit into a stocking.'

'Come and see, come and see.' Scott was out of the car, shouting his excitement, and the dogs were barking hysterically in response. William emerged from the driver's side, leaned back on the car door and crossed his arms—a genie who'd produced magic and was now expecting appreciation. He was wearing jeans and a short-sleeved open-topped shirt. He looked...great. He must have stopped at a clothes shop, Meg thought, and then she thought *I kissed him*—and then Scott's excitement tugged her attention back to what was on the trailer

At the front of the trailer was a Mini Minor, the kind that had been almost the coolest car on the planet back in the seventies. Though maybe it hadn't been quite as cool as the Volkswagen Combi.

Um...what was she thinking? She hadn't even been born in the seventies. This Mini, however, looked as if it had been. It was truly derelict. The little red and rust-red car had no wheels, no glass in its front windscreen and its hood was missing. What looked like grass was sprouting from where the engine should be.

And tied on behind was part of another Mini, in even worse repair. Instead of suffering from neglect, this one looked as if it had been smashed from behind. The back had been squashed almost to the front.

There was also a pile of assorted bits tied on top, meaning the trailer looked like a mini wrecker's yard.

'It's William's Christmas present to us all,' Scott shouted and her boss beamed and she thought again—he looks great.

Denim made him look *so-o-o-o* sexy—but somehow she managed to give her hormones a mental slap and ventured off the veranda to see.

William's Christmas present to us all...

'We saw a sign just out of town.' Despite his bad leg, Scott was practically jigging his excitement. 'It was in a paddock and it said For Sale. And parts as well. The guy restores Minis but his wife's put her foot down. He has three finished Minis in his garage and two more to restore and his wife says the rest have to go. So he sold us this. Two cars'll make one. He says there's enough here to make a complete one. He reckons if I start now, by the time I get my licence I'll have it on the road. If I get it going before then, I can practice in the paddocks. I can phone him any time I want, and if I'm really stuck he's even offered to come out here to help.'

'He really will,' William said, still smiling. 'This won't be any work for either of you. I promise.' His lovely, lazy smile lit his face and Meg thought frantically she'd have to give those hormones another slap.

'I have faith,' he went on. 'This'll mean eventually the farm has two cars. By the way, we also went to the motor place in Curalo and bought bits for your wagon, Letty. Your exhaust pipe has to be replaced and the silencer and so does the carburettor. If it's okay with you, I might make a start this afternoon.'

'You...' Meg said, dazed.

'I can fix cars,' he said neutrally. 'And Scott would like to learn.'

'You want to fix my car?' Letty said, while Meg simply stood with her mouth open.

'If it's okay with you.'

'Marry me,' Letty said, and Scott and William laughed— only, for some reason, Meg had trouble laughing. The sight of her boss in jeans was disconcerting enough, but she was looking at Scott's flushed face and his shining happiness and she thought, why hadn't she thought of this?

Scott was practically stranded here on the farm. His bad leg left him isolated. There were so many days when he simply gazed at his computer, in misery and in loneliness.

He now had a car to make. And it was an original Mini...

Mickey would come, she thought, and more. This project would be a magnet. Scott's mates would come, as they had before the accident.

She was blinking back tears.

'What's wrong?' William demanded, watching her face and clearly confounded.

She sniffed and tried desperately to think of something to say. Something to do rather than kiss him again, which seemed an entirely logical thing to do, but some germ of common sense was holding her back.

'I...I wanted perfume,' she managed, and her little brother stared at her as if she was out of her mind.

'Perfume...when you could have these!'

'They're not very...girlie,' she said and somehow she managed to sound doleful and Scott realised she was joking and grinned and hugged her. Which was amazing all by itself. How long since her seriously self-conscious brother had hugged?

'I'll let you drive my car,' he offered, magnanimity at its finest. 'Second drive after me, the minute I get it going.'

'What an offer,' she said and sniffed again and hugged him back and then smiled across at William through unshed tears.

'Thank you, Santa,' she said.

'Think nothing of it,' he said in a voice she didn't recognise and then she thought, no, she did know what she was hearing.

Her normally businesslike boss was just a wee bit emotional himself.

* * *

It was time for milking. Letty and Meg milked because, 'I'm not interfering with this, even if I have to milk the whole herd,' Letty declared in wonder. Meg could only agree, for kids were arriving from everywhere. It seemed William had detoured past Mickey's with their load—'just to show him,' Scott had told them, and Mickey had sent out word, and before they knew it a team of adolescents was unloading the heap of Mini jumble into the unused shed behind the dairy.

When milking was done Meg checked on Millicent—the little heifer was thankfully showing no signs of calving—then went to investigate. The teenagers were surrounded by Mini parts. William was under Letty's car.

'Sorry. I know I said I'd milk, but Letty assured me she could and someone had to supervise…'

Some supervision. All she could see of William was his legs. He was in his borrowed overalls again and his gumboots.

On the other side of the shed teenagers were happily dismantling the wreck, labelling pieces with Letty's preserving stickers. She had a bunch of gloriously happy teenagers, and the guy who'd caused it all to happen was apologising. Meg stared down at her boss's legs and thought she could totally understand where Letty's proposal had come from.

And she'd never realised until now how sexy a pair of grease-covered legs could be.

'So… So where did you learn mechanics?' she managed.

'I told you. Powering up my father's golf cart.' His voice was muffled, but she was aware of an undercurrent of contentment.

'And the rest?'

'My parents were away a lot. They had enough cars to warrant hiring a mechanic. He taught me.'

'Nice guy,' Meg said, deflected from thinking about legs— or almost. She thought instead of gossip she'd read about this man, about how appalling his parents sounded, how lonely his childhood must have been. 'Did this mechanic have a name?'

'Mr Himmel.'

'Mr Himmel.' She grimaced at the formality. 'He called you Mr McMaster?'

'Of course. Can you pass me under the tension wrench?'

'Tension wrench?'

'On the left with the blue handle.'

'That's a tension wrench?'

'And you a dairy farmer and all.'

'Dairy farmers aren't necessarily mechanics. Plus I'm a commerce graduate. And a PA.'

'Right, I forgot,' he said, but absently, and she knew his attention was on whatever he needed the tension wrench for.

She watched his legs for a little. His attention was totally on the car.

She watched the boys for a little. Their attention was totally on the car.

Guys doing guy stuff.

Befuddled, she headed back to the dairy, where Letty was sluicing. They cleaned almost in silence but she was aware that Letty kept glancing at her.

'What?' Meg said at last, exasperated.

'He's lovely.'

'So why are you looking at me?' She sighed. 'Anyway, he's not lovely. He's covered in grease.'

'You know what I mean.'

'Okay, I do,' she admitted. 'But you know who he is, so you can stop looking at me like you think I should do something about it. He's William McMaster, one of the wealthiest men on the planet. He's my boss and I have one of the best jobs in the world. If you think I'm messing with it by thinking he's lovely…'

'I suppose it would mess with it,' Letty said. 'Falling for the boss...'

'It'd be a disaster.'

'I don't know how you haven't before.'

'Because I've never seen him in overalls before.'

'They do make a man look sexy,' Letty said thoughtfully. 'That and carrying a grease gun. My Jack was always attached to a grease gun. Mind, once I had to get the grease off his clothes the novelty pretty soon wore off.' She sighed but then she brightened. 'But times have changed. Domestic equality and all that. He could get his own grease off.'

'You're seriously suggesting William McMaster could do his own laundry?' Meg even managed a chuckle. The idea merited a chuckle.

As was thinking of those legs, sticking out from under Letty's car. As was thinking that William McMaster was sexy.

Legs or not, even if the man carries a grease gun, he's still my boss, she told herself. A good servant knows her place. Just plaster that message across your box of hormones and leave it there.

They ate dinner on the run. The boys were in no hurry to go home. At dusk they took off, pack-like, whooping away on their bicycles, and Meg knew they'd be back first thing in the morning.

This was priceless.

Scott was almost asleep on his feet, but lit up almost as much as the Christmas tree in the sitting room. He fell into bed happier than she'd seen him for years.

Letty commandeered William to take him over to the shed to show her what he was doing with her car. Meg headed out behind the hay shed. Millicent was still doing little of interest, the small fawn and white cow chewing her cud and gazing placidly out at the fading sunset.

'Mind if I share your sunset?' she asked, and Millicent turned her huge bovine eyes on her and seemed to ask a question.

'He's only here until Monday. Then it's back to normal,' Meg said, as if Millicent really was asking the question. Only what was the question? And what was normal?

She hitched herself up on the fence and started sunset-gazing. But she wasn't seeing sunset. 'This is just a hiccup in our lives,' she said out loud. 'But it's a great hiccup.'

She was under no illusion as to how big a deal this was. Ever since the accident Scotty's mates had been drifting away. They were nice kids. They included him when they could, but increasingly he was off their radar.

Today they'd returned and they'd hated leaving. Here was a project designed to keep kids happy for months, if not years. A project with a working car at the end of it… A Mini. They'd be back and back and back.

And it was all down to William. William of the sexy legs. William of the sexy…everything.

And suddenly, inexplicably, she was tearing up. She sniffed and Millicent pushed her great wet nose under her arm as if in sympathy.

'Yeah, you'd know about men,' she retorted. 'Of all the dumb blondes…'

'Who's a dumb blonde?'

She hadn't heard him approach. He moved like a panther, she thought, startled. He was long and lithe and silent as the night. He leaned against her fence, and she had to hitch along a bit so he could climb up and sit beside her.

'Dumb blonde?' he said again.

'Meet Millicent,' she said. 'Dumb adolescent blonde.'

'That not a kind thing to say about an obviously sweet cow.'

'She's oversexed,' Meg said darkly, struggling not to react to the way his body brushed against hers. There was plenty of room. Why did he need to sit so close?

'Really?' It was William's turn to sound startled.

'Really.'

'So how do you tell if a cow is oversexed?'

'She got out of her paddock,' she explained. 'Not only did she get out, she got in again. We finally found her in our next door neighbour's bull paddock. Now she's pregnant and she's too young to have babies but that's what she's having, any day now. Letty's worried sick.'

'What's to worry about?'

'We don't know which bull it was.'

'You don't know which bull...'

'It could have been one of three.'

'You're telling me she's...loose?' he demanded, and she giggled and swayed on her perch and he put a hand out to steady her. He shifted closer and held on around the waist, making sure she was secure. She waited for him to let her go—but he didn't.

'So tell me all,' he demanded, and she thought, do you know what the feel of your arm around my waist is doing to me? Obviously not or it'd be gone in a flash.

Maybe she should tell him.

Or not.

She had to do something. She was getting close to melting here. 'I think you'd better let me go—Mr McMaster,' she managed, and he did. He shifted away a little, without comment, as if it meant nothing. As if holding her hadn't caused him any sort of reaction. Nothing like the sizzle that had just jolted through her.

'So are we waiting for the baby to be born so we can take DNA samples and enforce a paternity suit?' he asked, and they were talking about Millicent. Of course they were.

'Maybe not.' She was totally discombobulated. It wasn't just the feel of his arm. It was so much more. 'I… one of the bulls is a Murray Grey.'

'That's bad?'

'If you're a Friesian crossed with a Jersey, it's very bad. Have you ever met a Murray Grey?'

'I can't say I have.'

'They're about half Millicent's size again. She's still un-derdeveloped. If we'd found her straight away we could have done something, but she got out and we lost her and didn't find her for ages. What must have happened was that she got out onto the road, wandered along happily, we suspect, looking for bulls because she's that sort of girl. Whoever found her must have shooed her through the nearest gate to get her off the road—which, of course, happened to be Rod Palmer's bull paddock. There was plenty of feed in the paddock. It's hilly and mostly out of sight of the road and Rod lets his bulls be until he needs them. So Millicent might have been enjoying herself for quite a while. She certainly seemed content when Rod finally found her and called us.'

'Uh-oh,' he said. 'So now?'

'So now she's in the house paddock while we wait for the birth. Signs are any day now. I hope to heaven she doesn't drop over Christmas because there's no way we'll get a vet.' Then a thought occurred and she eyed him with hope. 'As well as cars… You didn't have a houseful of pets you practised on when you were a kid as well?' she enquired. 'Maybe a cow or two, and a resident vet?'

'Nary a goldfish.'

'Not even a dog?' she demanded, startled.

'My family don't do pets.'

'But you like them.'

'Just because I patted Killer…'

'No, but you do. When we're out on site… Every time we meet a dog you talk to it. You should have one.'

'And leave him in my Manhattan apartment alone, for months at a time?'

'You have staff. Is Mr Himmel still around?'

'Long gone.' That was said bleakly and she thought—don't go there. She was pushing past anywhere that was her business. Move on.

But move on where? Move onto where she wanted to go? Why not?

'So…so do you need to go over to Jenny's again later?' she managed.

'Jenny's?'

'Mickey's. To make more phone calls.'

'I rang Elinor while I was in Curalo.'

Elinor. First name. The word hung between them, loaded with unknowns.

Leave it, she thought, but then she thought if she was Letty she'd ask. She swung her legs against the fence rails and tried to look nonchalant. As if this was a lightweight question.

'So the gossip rags haven't caught up with Elinor?'

'I hope they never do.' It was said with such vehemence that she blinked.

'Um…it's serious then?'

He seemed disconcerted but then he shrugged. 'You could say that.'

'I'm sorry you'll miss Christmas with her, then.'

'I'm sorry, too.' He swung himself down from the fence and she knew the question had messed with whatever calm he'd been feeling. 'I believe I need to get that carburettor back in. Without it, we're dependent on the tractor as emergency transport so I'm not going to bed before it's in working order. It's okay. Twenty minutes work, tops. I'm not being a martyr.' He glanced down at his overalls and he smiled, with unmistakable all-boy satisfaction. 'I haven't looked this greasy since I was Scott's age. It feels great.'

'You are great,' she said as he reached up and took her by the waist and lifted her down to join him. He should let her go. He didn't.

'So are you.'

Uh-oh.

Keep it light, she told herself. *Keep it light.* 'If our office staff could see us now they'd have kittens,' she managed.

'Or a cameraman.'

The paparazzi. That was an appalling thought. She could see the headlines now: *McMaster Trapped with Secretary in Rural Hideway...* What would the unknown Elinor say if she saw such a headline?

'Does Elinor know you're stuck with me?' He was still holding her. She should step away—but she didn't.

'Yes,' he said.

'She doesn't mind?'

'She's upset for me. She knows I want to be home.'

For some reason that hurt, but she made herself respond. 'That's generous of Elinor.'

'She's a generous woman.'

What to say to that? And he was still holding her.

'I...I need to go to bed,' she managed and she tugged a little but still he didn't release her.

'Bed?'

'In case you hadn't noticed, it's nine, which is the witching hour when milking starts at five.'

'So you don't look forward to your morning milk?' he teased.

He was so close... She was having trouble making her voice work but she had to try. 'Getting up at five... Ugh,' she said. 'But while I'm here it's normal. For lots of people it's normal. You get up at five to check on your trade indices all the time. You don't mind.'

'So what do you want to do at five?'

'Sleep!'

He smiled, then put his head on one side, considering. 'So why stay on here? You're putting your life on hold for your little brother.'

'I haven't noticed much life-holding.'

'Where's the social life? When you work with me I demand twenty-four seven commitment. Then you come here and it seems the same. Milking from five to nine and milking from three to seven. Where's time for Meg in that?'

He sounded concerned, and that disconcerted her. He'd never sounded concerned. Their relationship was businesslike.

It had to stay that way.

'I have wild lunches,' she told him.

'Right.' He was watching her in a way that disturbed her. As if he was trying to figure her out.

'So…boyfriend?' he asked and she winced. Ouch. That'd do as far as personal questions went. He set his boundaries. She'd set hers.

'That's not your territory, Mr McMaster.' She tugged back and this time he did let her go. She made to turn away but his next question stopped her.

'Do you like working for me?'

That was an easy one. 'I love it.'

'Why?'

She hesitated. He was watching her in the fading light, and she knew her answer meant something to him.

'It's smart work,' she said slowly. 'I never know what my day's going to hold. I need to use my brain, and I love it that you treat me like I can.'

'Like you can what?'

'Rise to any challenge.' She managed a smile at that. 'Except get you home for Christmas.'

He didn't smile back. Silence. The sun had sunk well over the horizon and the light was disappearing fast. The night was warm and still. Millicent was right beside them by the fence, oozing the contentment of a soon-to-be mum who had everything she wanted in life.

Except she didn't have her bull, Meg thought, and then thought what was she thinking? *Her bull?*

'Bed,' she said.

'Sounds good,' he said and she blushed and stepped away so fast she tripped on her own feet. He put out a hand to catch her but she staggered and grabbed the fence and maintained her distance.

'Is there anything else you need?' she asked, stammering.

'I don't believe so.' He was laughing, she thought—not obviously, but there was laughter behind his eyes. 'So do we have a date with a hundred cows at five in the morning?'

'I can't believe you offered to milk.'

'It will be my pleasure.'

'In lieu of the world's trade indices.'

'In lieu of trade indices.' He hesitated. 'I really don't mind getting up early,' he told her. 'If you need to sleep... I wish I could milk them for you.'

He was serious.

'Yeah, well, I do have some affection for the cows,' she managed. 'Though it's a wonderful offer...' She took a deep breath. 'As was buying Scott the car. I'd like to pay.'

'Get off your high horse, Jardine.'

'It's not my high horse, it's my dignity,' she said with as much dignity as she could muster. 'By which I take it that you won't let me. In which case I'm very, very grateful. So thank you, Mr McMaster, and goodnight.'

'William,' he said, and it was a snap.

'William, then,' she said and met his gaze for as long as she dared—which wasn't very long at all.

'Sleep well,' he said and, before she knew what he was about, he reached out and touched her face. It was a feather touch, a fleeting brush of his finger against her cheek, but he might as well have kissed her. She raised her hand to her cheek as if he'd applied heat. Maybe he had.

'Sleep...sleep well yourself,' she whispered.

'I'll see what I can do,' he said. 'And Meg?'

'Yes?'

'Thank you for rising to my challenges. I appreciate it.'

He was still so close. She desperately wanted him to touch her again. She stood and stared up at him, but there was nothing to say.

She desperately wanted him to kiss her.

And where would businesslike be after that?

'Good...goodnight,' she managed, and then she turned and left him standing in the darkness leaning against a pregnant cow.

She knew that he watched her all the way back to the house.

He should move. He still had to get the carburettor in and he did have to get up at the same time as she did. Instead, he watched Meg's retreating figure and when she disappeared he stood and stared at the darkened house, lit only by its ridiculous decorations. Santa's legs were lurching at an even more alarming rate.

That was the morning's job, he decided. He'd do it after milking. Then he'd replace Letty's exhaust pipe. Then he'd help Scott with the Mini. He was looking forward to each of them.

So much for feeling trapped.

This was a weird sensation. The McMaster family business, a vast mining conglomerate, had been founded by his grandfather. William's father hadn't wanted to go near the business. His grandfather, however, had found his retiring grandson to be intelligent and biddable, and he'd thrown William in at the deep end.

That had been okay by William. He enjoyed the cut and thrust of the business world and in a way it made up for the lack of affection in his family. His grandfather had approved of him when he was doing well for the company, and on his grandfather's death he'd simply kept on with what he was good at. That was what the world expected. It was what he expected of himself.

But here... He'd forgotten how much he loved pulling a car apart. He'd loved his time with Scott.

As he'd love returning to Manhattan, he reminded himself.

When he finally arrived at Elinor's apartment, his reception would be just as crazy as Meg's had been. Or maybe not quite, he conceded. Ned was six years old and his little sister was four. They could bounce but they didn't quite equate to a five-dog pack, a grandma and a brother. And Elinor... Her smile would be as warm as it was possible for a smile to be, but Elinor was a sixty-two-year-old foster mother and she welcomed the world.

Like Letty.

Like Meg, too.

No. Don't think about Meg, he told himself. It's making you crazy. Meg was his PA. He was leaving in two days and he did not want to mess with their employer/employee relationship.

The problem was, though, that he was no longer able to think of her purely as his employee.

He'd called her Meg.

Don't think about her, he told himself again sharply as he headed for the shed. Think about people he could justifiably be attached to.

Like Elinor. Elinor expected nothing, which was just the way he liked it.

He'd been introduced to Elinor two years back, at the launch of New York's Foster-Friends programme. The programme was designed to give support to those who put their lives on hold for kids in need. He'd been approached to be a sponsor, he'd met Elinor at the launch and he'd been sucked right in by her commitment. Elinor was everything he wasn't—warm, devoted and passionate about Pip and Ned, the two kids in her care.

Tentatively, he'd suggested helping a little himself. Part-time commitment. Walking away when he needed to. It sounded… feasible. 'I'm not often available' he'd said and Elinor had beamed as if he were promising the world.

'Anything's better than what these two have been getting up to now,' she'd said simply. 'It breaks my heart their Mama won't put them up for adoption and they so need a Papa. You come when you can and you leave the rest to me.'

The thought of letting them down at Christmas had made him feel ill, but Elinor's big-hearted wisdom had come straight back at him.

'I have a turkey. We have candy and paper lanterns and a tree. We're going out today to see the fancy shop windows and then the kids are visiting Santa. You get home when you can and we'll love to see you, but don't you worry about us, Mr McMaster. We'll do fine.'

The relationship suited him fine. Elinor didn't depend on him. She gave her heart to the kids.

As Meg had given her heart to her half brother, and to a woman who wasn't really her grandmother.

Meg was a giver. His cool, clinical PA was just like

Elinor, and for some reason the thought had the capacity to scare him.

Why?

He didn't want to think about why. He reached the shed but he paused before flicking on the lights and going inside. He glanced back at the house—where Meg was.

Don't think about Meg.

Those Santa legs were getting on his nerves. Maybe he should try and fix them now.

And fall off the roof in the dark. They'd find him tomorrow, tangled in flashing Christmas lights, a cloud of self-pity hanging round his head.

'So maybe you'd better go to bed and stop thinking about fixing things,' he told himself.

Things? Plural?

What else needed to be fixed?

'Letty's car, the Mini and Santa's legs,' he said out loud. 'What else is there? Why would I want anything in my world to change?'

What indeed?

The Santa legs were seriously disconcerting. He turned his gaze upward where a million stars hung in the sky, brighter than he'd ever seen them.

'There are too many stars out here,' he told himself. 'They make a man disoriented. The world's the wrong way up. I've had enough.'

He flicked on the lights and went inside, but outside he knew the stars stayed hanging. Still the wrong way up.

They'd be the wrong way up until he could get out of here. Which should be soon.

Which had to be soon, because he was having trouble remembering what the right way up looked like.

* * *

She lay in her bed and she thought—I am in so much trouble.

Her boss wore jeans. He looked great with greasy hands. He smiled at her…

Do not fall in love with your boss.

How not to?

It's simply a crush, she told herself desperately. He's been touted as one of the most eligible bachelors in the world. When he finally smiles at you like you're a woman—like you're a friend—of course you're going to fall for him.

Any woman would.

So any woman must not make a fool of herself. Any woman had to remember that he moved in a different world to hers, that he was in Australia for three months of the year at the most and the rest he was with…

A woman called Elinor in Manhattan?

She so badly wanted the Internet. She wanted to check out any rumours. W S McMaster and a woman called Elinor.

You have it bad, she told the ceiling and when the door wobbled a little bit on its hinges and slowly opened she almost stopped breathing. Was it…?

Killer. Her dog had obviously decided his duty was with her rather than as one of Scotty's pack. He nosed her hand and then climbed laboriously up onto her bed, making hard work out of what was, for Killer, hardly a step.

'Your mistress is in trouble,' she told him and he whumped down on top of her and she had to shove him away a bit so she could breathe. He promptly turned and tried to lick her.

'Okay, you're the only man in my life. And if I was to think about admitting another one…'

Another lick, this time longer

'Yeah, no room, you're right. Forget it. We have to go to sleep. There's milking in the morning and tomorrow it's Christmas Eve.'

She hadn't written her Santa list. The thought came from nowhere. As a little girl, that was the major job before Christmas. In truth, as a child she'd usually started her Santa list in November.

'Well, it's no use asking for what I want now,' she told Killer and then she heard what she'd said and she winced.

But it was true. She did want it.

'Me and every single woman in the known universe,' she muttered. 'Especially someone called Elinor. Killer, get off me and let me go to sleep.'

She thought Elinor was his woman.

He lay and stared up at the attic ceiling and thought through the events of the day—and that was the fact that stood out.

He hadn't lied to her. But he had let her think…

'Defence,' he told the darkness and thought—how conceited was that? As if she was going to jump him…

He'd had women trying to jump him before. He knew how to defend himself.

He wasn't the least worried about Meg overstepping the line.

The line.

Meg.

See, there was the problem, he told himself. He'd let himself call her Meg. He'd let himself think about her as Meg. She was his employee, his wonderful, efficient PA. All he had to do was go back to thinking of her as Miss Jardine and all would be well.

But she'd felt…

And there was another problem. He could give his head all the orders he liked, but his body was another matter entirely. When he'd tugged her down from the fence she'd fallen against him. Her body had felt soft, pliable, curving into him, even if only for a fraction of a second before she'd tugged away. And she smelled of something he couldn't identify. Not perfume, he thought, and he knew most, but something else. Citrusy, clean...

She'd spent most of the day surrounded by cows. How could she smell clean?

She did, and this wasn't getting him anywhere. He needed to sleep. He had a big day tomorrow, milking cows, fixing things... Trying not to think about Meg.

Miss Jardine.

Why not think of her? It was a tiny voice, insidious, starting from nowhere.

Because you don't.

The thought of Hannah was suddenly with him, Hannah, holding him, loving him, and suddenly...not there. The pain had been unbelievable.

His world was hard. He had no illusions as to what wealth could do to people, marriages, relationships. Wealth had destroyed his parents, turned them into something ugly, surrounded by sycophants in their old age. It took enormous self-control to stop himself from being sucked down the same path.

And he had no idea how to cope with an emotional connection.

It didn't matter. His work was satisfying. His life was satisfying, and if there were spaces...Elinor and the kids were enough.

They took what he had to give.

Maybe Meg...

'Don't even go there,' he said savagely into the night. 'You're not as selfish as that. She deserves so much more.'

CHAPTER SIX

IT TOOK Meg a while to wake up on milking mornings. She liked working in silence for the first half hour or so, and that suited the cows. They usually seemed to be half asleep too, ridding themselves of their load of milk before getting on with their daily task of grazing, snoozing and making more.

But, eventually, Meg woke up. Whether she was working with Letty or Kerrie, by the time milking ended she usually had the radio on, she was chatting to whoever was around, singing along with the radio; even the cows seemed more cheerful.

But not this morning. Her boss seemed to have left his bed on the wrong side. He worked methodically, swabbing, attaching cups, releasing cows from the bales, but answering any ventured conversation with monosyllables. Yes, no, and nothing more was forthcoming.

It was probably for the best, Meg decided as they worked on. Yesterday had threatened to get out of hand. She wasn't quite sure what it was that was getting out of hand, but whatever it was scared her. She knew enough to retreat now into her own world and let W S McMaster get on with his.

It was disconcerting, though. With milking finished, William handled the hose with none of yesterday's enjoyment. She found herself getting irritated, and when Craig arrived to pick up the milk and gestured towards William and said, 'So who's the boyfriend?' she was able to shake her head without even raising colour. Who'd want someone like this for a boyfriend?

'He's someone I work with. He's stuck here because of the airline strike.'

'And he bought the kid the Minis?' It seemed the whole district knew about the Minis. Craig's son had been under the car pile last night and would be back here this morning.

'Yeah.'

'Good move,' he said approvingly. He glanced across at William, obviously aching to talk cars, but William was concentrating on getting the yard hosed and nothing was distracting him. 'Seemed happier yesterday,' he noted.

'He's homesick.'

'Wife? Kids?'

'No.'

'Then what's he whinging about?' Craig demanded. He yelled over to William, 'Hey, Will. Merry Christmas. There's no dairy pick-up tomorrow, so have a good one.'

William raised a hand in a slight salute and went on hosing. Craig departed and Meg surveyed her boss carefully.

'We've offended you?'

He shrugged.

Oh, enough. 'It's Christmas Eve,' she said. 'Lighten up.'

'I'll finish here. You go do something else. Don't you have to stuff a turkey or something?'

'Right,' she said and stalked out of the yard, really irritated now. She was hungry. She'd intended to wait for William before she ate breakfast, but he could eat his toast alone.

She detoured via Millicent, and that made her pause. Millicent was standing in the middle of the home paddock, her back arched a little and her tail held high. Uh-oh. When Meg slipped through the rails and crossed to check, the cow relaxed and let Meg rub her nose, but Meg thought the calf would be here soon, today or tomorrow.

Here was another factor to complicate her Christmas. Letty would worry all day.

Every now and then a cow came along you got fond of. Millicent was one of those. Born after a difficult labour, she'd been a weakling calf. A hard-headed dairy farmer would have sold her straight away. Letty, however, had argued the pros and cons with herself for a week while tending to her like a human baby, and after a week she'd decided she had potential.

She'd named her before she'd decided to name the rest of the herd, and she'd been gutted when she'd been lost. Finding her had been a joy.

'So let's do this right for Letty,' Meg told her and went and fetched her a bucket of chaff and shooed her closer to the trough. 'No complications for Christmas.'

There was nothing more she could do now, though. Labour in cows didn't require a support person, at least in the early stages.

Breakfast. Hunger. And don't think about William, she told herself; he was yet another complication she didn't need.

And then a scream split the morning, a scream so high and terrified Meg's heart seemed to stop. She forgot all about William, forgot about Millicent's complications, and she started to run.

The concrete was as clean as he could make it. No speck of dirt was escaping his eagle eye this morning and he finally turned off the tap with regret. Move on to the next thing fast, he thought. He had today and tomorrow to get through while keeping things businesslike.

Meg would be in the kitchen, having breakfast. Yesterday he'd watched her eat toast. Before yesterday he'd never watched her eat toast. Yes, he travelled with her often, but when he did he ordered breakfast in his room. He wasted less time that way.

But yesterday he'd decided he liked watching her eat breakfast. Dumb or not, it wasn't a bad way to waste time.

A man could waste a lot of time watching Meg.

And that was exactly what he was trying not to think. He wound the hose back onto the reel with more force than was necessary and thought he'd see if Scott was in the shed yet. It was after eight. He could talk to Scott for a while and then maybe Meg would be finished in the kitchen.

What sort of coward was he? What was to be afraid of, watching Meg eat toast?

Meg. Miss Jardine.

Meg.

He sighed and ran his hand through his hair. Two days…

He could do this. He turned towards the house, irritated with himself. All this needed was a bit of discipline. Containment.

And then…a scream.

Forget containment. He ran.

It was Letty. Where? Where?

As Meg neared the house Letty screamed again.

Dear God…

She was high up on the roof, right by the Santa chimney. Had she been trying to fix him? But now wasn't the time for questions. Letty was dangling from the ridge, tiny and frail and in deadly peril.

The roof had two inclines, the main one steep enough, but the attic gable rising even more steeply. The roof was old, the iron was rusting, and the capping on the high ridge had given way. Or was giving way. It hadn't given completely.

It was all that was holding Letty up.

Scotty burst out of the house as Meg arrived. 'Grandma!'

'She's on the roof.'

The capping tore again, just a little, iron scraping on iron. Letty lurched downward but somehow still held.

'Grandma,' Scott screamed, his voice breaking in terror. 'Hang on!'

Meg was too busy to scream. How had she climbed? The ladder… Where? By the gate.

But then William was beside her, reaching the ladder before she did. 'Hold it,' he snapped. 'Scott, hold the other side.'

The capping tore more, and Letty lurched again.

'Letty, hold on,' William ordered her, in a voice that brooked no argument. 'Fingernails if you must, but do not let go. I'm coming.'

'H…hurry.'

He was already climbing. 'Keep still.'

How could you defy that voice? Why would you?

Nobody moved. Meg and Scott held to the ladder as if their lives depended on it.

Their lives didn't. Letty's did, and so did William's.

The roof was high pitched, curved, dangerous, and the ladder only reached part way to the top ridge. William clambered over the main eaves as if they weren't there. It was impossible to climb further, Meg thought numbly from underneath. The second gable was far too steep—but somehow William was doing it.

'You'll fall,' she faltered.

'Not me,' he said, finding footholds she knew couldn't exist. 'Mountaineering 101—Basic skills for your modern businessman. Watch and wonder.'

She watched, and yes, she wondered, but it wasn't admiration she was feeling. It was blind terror.

Please. Please.

And then somehow, unbelievably, William was on the upper ridge, edging himself toward Letty. Santa's sleigh was between them. He shoved; it tumbled back behind the house and no one noticed its going.

He edged closer…closer…while below him Meg and Scott forgot to breathe.

He'd reached her. He was steadying, stabilising himself over the ridge, grasping Letty's wrists and holding.

He had her.

'Don't move. Just lie limp and let me pull you up.'

Scotty choked on a sob. Meg gripped his hand and held, taking comfort as well as giving it. Letty wasn't safe yet. William was still balanced on a ridge with an already broken capping.

The ladder only reached to the eaves of the main roof, so what now? William might be able to climb up like a cat burglar. It was impossible that he climb down holding Letty.

'Meg?'

'Y…yes?'

'I can't get us down,' he told her. 'Not the way I came up. If I overbalance we'll both go.'

She knew it. They needed the fire brigade, she thought. They needed help.

They had no phone. The nearest neighbour was a mile away, but William already knew that.

'I'm buying you a satellite phone for Christmas,' he muttered. 'If it costs a million bucks you're still having one.' He had Letty solidly under the arms now and was hauling her upward like a limp doll. 'So Letty, are you going to argue?'

'N…No.'

'Good woman.' One last heave and he had her on the ridge, into his arms.

She was safe, Meg thought. Or…safeish. With the capping gone the whole attic roof looked unstable but at least Letty was no longer dangling.

But… Her wrist looked hurt. She could see a crimson stain from here. She was losing blood?

William was inching backward along the ridge, heading for the chimney. He could lean on the bricks. Safeish was turning to safe.

Sort of. Until he came to get her down.

'This cut's not looking good,' he said, almost conversationally, and Meg thought he was trying not to scare Letty. But she knew this voice. It meant he wanted action, fast. He tugged Letty hard against him, leaned back against the chimney to make them both stable, then ripped the sleeve from his overalls, as if it was gauze instead of industrial-strength cotton. He wound the fabric round her arm and held her close.

'So how did you get up here?' he asked.

Letty didn't answer. Not a good sign.

He stared downward, seemingly as mystified as Meg. That Letty could have scrambled up the way he had seemed incredible.

'There…there's another ladder,' Scott ventured. He was shaking, and Meg's hand firmed over his.

'Another ladder?'

'When I put the sleigh up I used two.'

'You used two…'

'It fell,' Letty muttered, her voice barely above a whisper. 'As I reached the top. I grabbed, but it went and then I grabbed the capping.'

Meg was no longer listening. She was searching the undergrowth, and here it was. Another ladder, buried behind the banksias.

Scott and Letty had both climbed up on this ancient roof using two ladders. Alone.

Were they out of their minds?

She shouldn't have left them. She should've been here. She should…

Just get a grip, she told herself. Blame needed to wait.

'I'll get the ladder back up,' she called to William. 'Hold on.'

There was no time for hesitation. She moved the main ladder along the wall so it was wedged against the yard gate, so Scott could hold it steady by himself. Then she headed up, tugging the smaller ladder with her.

'Meg…' William sounded appalled. 'What do you think you're doing?'

'Scott's done it. Letty's done it. If all of my stupid family is intent on self destruction I might as well join them. There's no alternative.'

There wasn't. He knew there wasn't.

'You fall and you're fired,' he snapped.

'That's right. Resort to threats under pressure. You fall and I quit,' she snapped back, and caught the flash of a rueful smile.

But… How had Letty and Scotty done this, she thought, as she struggled upward. They'd climbed the first ladder dragging the next, each doing it alone?

She'd looked at Santa's legs last night and she'd thought the same as Letty obviously had—that she'd have a go at fixing him. But Letty was in her seventies, and that Scott could have tried with his leg in a brace…

She shuddered and she paused, half way up the ladder.

'You can do it,' William said strongly and she looked up and met his gaze and took a deep breath.

During the years she'd worked for William she'd been given the most extraordinary orders. She'd done the most extraordinary things.

You can do it.

She loved working for William.

You fall and you're fired.

What did he think she was? A wuss? She climbed on.

She reached the first eave. She balanced herself, took a deep breath and swung the second ladder up to the next eave.

'No,' William said.

'No?'

'It won't hold.' He sounded calm now, back in control. He'd obviously been using the time while she struggled to think the scenario through. 'I can see where it fell. The guttering's broken and there's no guarantee it won't break again. You'll need to lie a plank along its length so the ladder's weight's on half a dozen fastenings instead of one.'

'I'll get a plank,' Scott said.

'Scott!' William's voice would have stopped an army.

'What?'

'Let that ladder go before your sister's down and you're fired, too. Meg, leave the ladder where it is and go find the plank with Scott. You do this together. My way or not at all.'

Meg looked at her boss. He looked straight back.

'Let's do what the man says,' she told her little brother. 'He's the boss.'

They found a beam, ten foot long. Scott heaved from below and she tugged. She laid it along the length of guttering. She shifted the second ladder so it was balanced on the midpoint and it was as safe as they could make it. Done.

All William had to do was edge Letty back along the ridge—and let Meg take her down.

'You can't.' William's voice was agonised as they faced this final step, but he knew the facts. Meg was five foot five; he was six feet two. He weighed at least forty pounds more than she did. Everything depended on the guttering holding.

Letty couldn't climb herself. It was Meg who'd support Letty on the way down.

Slowly William edged back along the ridge, lifting Letty

a little at each move. She was so limp, Meg thought. She couldn't get her down if she lost consciousness. But…

'I'm saving my strength,' Letty whispered.

'You're a woman with intelligence as well as courage,' William said, and he met Meg's gaze, and she thought…

She thought…

Yeah, well, there wasn't a lot of use going down that path. Of all the inappropriate things to think right now. He looked lean and mean and dangerous. He had torn overalls, blood-stained chest, one arm bared. His expression was grim and focussed. He was totally intent on what he was doing. He looked… He looked…

She knew how he looked. She also knew how he was making her feel, and somehow it made things…

Scarier? That she'd decided she loved a man who was balanced on a crumbling ridge, with her injured grandmother in his arms and her little brother underneath, and if they fell…

Um…get a grip.

She gripped.

William was moving so slowly there was no risk of him overbalancing. He was shifting Letty a few inches at a time.

The wait was interminable.

'I have you steady.' It was Scott from underneath them. He'd climbed the first ladder and was holding the second.

This was safer—except it meant Scotty was right beneath her.

'Scott…' she started and she knew her voice quavered.

'Scott's fine. No one's going to fall,' William said. It was his 'no one's going home until this is sorted' voice. Meg blinked. Okay, she couldn't defy him on this one.

'Letty, you need to trust us all,' William said. 'Meg will catch your legs while you find a footing on the ladder. She'll be right under you, pressing you into the rungs. You'll hold as best you can with one hand. That's all you'll need. Meg will be guiding your feet, holding you firm. Don't release the first rung until you feel totally stable; stable enough to reach under for the next. If you can't do it then stop until you feel you can. There's no rush. We have all the time in the world.'

All the time in the world. Except Letty looked dreadful. If she fainted...

If she fainted then Meg would catch her and hold her and somehow get her down. No one's going to fall. The guy in the bloodstained overalls had said so.

'As soon as you have her I'll slide down the ridge the way I came up,' William said. 'I'll be beneath you.'

'What, slide and jump?' Meg retorted. 'You want a broken leg? Scotty's underneath and he'll do any catching.'

'I will,' Scott said, and Meg looked up and met William's gaze and saw agony. William McMaster depended on no one. For him to depend on a kid like Scott...

No choice. No one's going to fall.

And somehow no one did. Somehow William got a limp and trembling Letty onto Meg's ladder. Somehow Meg held her, guiding her every step of the way. Somehow they climbed down, rung after rung.

'Women are awesome,' Letty muttered as they reached the lower guttering and manoeuvred across to the next ladder. Meg even managed a smile.

'You bet. You ready for the next bit, Grandma?'

'Bring it on.' Letty's voice might be a thready whisper but her spirit was indomitable.

And then it was done. As they reached the ground Letty sagged but Scott was there. It was Scott who lifted his grandmother from the ladder. He had his Grandma in his arms, and then Meg was there, too, hugging them both.

And William was down, as well. He stood back, and Meg saw him over Letty's head, and she reached out and tugged him in as well. Her big, bloodstained hero. Her boss.

William.

They hugged together. Sandwich squeeze, she'd called this when she was little, when the family was celebrating, or something dreadful had happened, or sometimes simply because they could. Because they were family.

And this felt the same. It felt... Family?

Except William wasn't. She knew he wasn't, so it shouldn't hurt when he was the first to pull away.

It did. Even though he must.

'Let's have a look at that arm,' William said in a voice that was none too steady, and she knew he was feeling the whole gamut of emotions she was feeling. Only maybe not the family one.

There was a woman called Elinor?

Letty's knees had given completely. Scott brought cushions and blankets while Meg and William assessed the damage as best they could. Letty's arm was bound tightly with William's sleeve, but the crimson bloom was spreading.

'I don't think we should disturb it,' William said. 'Where's the nearest hospital.'

'I'm not going to hospital,' Letty quavered and for an answer William simply scooped her up, blankets and all.

'Car keys,' he snapped at Meg. 'You sit in the back seat with your grandmother. Scott, are you coming?'

Someone had turned into the drive. Mickey and his Dad, Meg thought, recognising the car, come to play with the Minis.

'Maybe...maybe I should stay,' Scott managed and then tried to get his voice down a quaver or two. 'I...Mickey can help me clean up.'

That Letty hadn't squeaked a second protest was scary, but William had her in his arms, heading for the car, and Meg could spare a moment to think things through. Scott loathed hospitals, for good reason. She could see he was torn. She needed to give him a reason to stay, and she had one. One pregnant cow.

'I need you to keep an eye on Millicent,' she said.

'Why?'

'She's showing the first signs of calving.'

'My Millicent...' Letty squeaked over William's shoulder.

'Your Millicent,' Meg retorted. 'Who's staying in the care of your grandson, and Mickey and Mickey's Dad. There's two for you and three for Millicent. So who's arguing, Grandma?'

'No one's arguing,' William said. 'Let's go.'

CHAPTER SEVEN

THE gash on her arm was deep and jagged. The doctors wanted to keep Letty in overnight, an option she wouldn't consider.

'Just pull it together and let me go. I have a turkey to stuff.'

Finally, they conceded that she could go home, but only after they were sure she was okay. 'She's lost a lot of blood, she's elderly and she's shocked,' the doctor on duty told them as they wheeled her off to Theatre. 'We'll tie her down for a couple of hours to make sure there aren't complications. Can you wait?'

'We can wait,' William said and he and Meg went to sit in the waiting room. Meg picked up a glossy magazine and stared sightlessly at its pages.

He shouldn't go near her, William decided.

Her hands were still shaking.

How could he not go to her? He moved to the seat next to hers and touched her hand.

She put her magazine down and blinked back tears.

So much for not going near her. He put his arm round her and tugged her close.

Her whole body was shaking.

'It's okay. Baby, it's okay.'

'I'm not…' She gulped and tried to pull away. 'I'm not b… baby.'

'Miss Jardine, it's okay,' he said, and pulled her closer still.

That brought a chuckle, but a watery one. She sniffed and reached for a tissue in her overalls pocket. She blew her nose, hard, and he thought, how could he go back to calling her Miss Jardine? This wasn't his super-efficient PA. This was someone he no longer knew.

Or maybe… Maybe it was just that he hadn't known his super-efficient PA, because it was starting to feel as if he did know this woman, and he wanted to know more.

'If…if the paparazzi could see us now,' she muttered and he winced. What a thing to think.

They'd come straight from the cow yard. They'd been filthy to begin with and Letty's blood had added a layer that was truly appalling.

'I think the chances of me being recognised are about zip,' he said. 'We're safe.'

'We are,' she whispered. 'Thanks to you. How did you ever get up on that roof?'

'I have skills you can't even begin to imagine,' he said, trying to make her smile.

'Can you fix Santa when we get home?'

'What?' He looked at her and discovered she was smiling—she was joking. She was still shaking but there was no way she was sinking into self-pity.

'I have a better idea,' he said unsteadily. 'Let's toss a grenade into the fireplace and blast him right out of there. All I've seen so far have been legs. A life without a head can't be all that satisfying. Let's put him out of his misery.'

She choked on something that could be a bubble of laughter or it could be tears, he couldn't decide which, and he hugged her closer and he simply held.

Eventually, the tremors stopped. He didn't let her go,

though. It felt okay to sit here and hold her—as if he had the right.

Did he want the right?

What sort of dumb thing was that to think? The shock of the morning must be getting to him.

She felt right, he thought. Holding her felt right.

But then a nurse came through the door and said, 'Miss Jardine?' and he was no longer holding her. His side felt cold without her there.

'Yes?' Meg was still frightened, he thought. She'd risen to face the nurse as if she was bracing for the worst.

She'd seen the worst, he thought. She'd have been here when her mother and stepfather were killed; when Scotty had been so appallingly injured.

She knew what happened when you let people get close.

He rose and stood beside her, and held her as the nurse approached.

But it was okay. 'Your brother's on the phone,' the nurse said. He watched as she took a deep steadying breath and nodded and moved away from the support of his arm and walked across to the nurses' station to take the call.

He watched her as she spoke. She seemed totally unconscious of how she looked. How many women did he know who could be so unaware of what they were wearing? His comment about her clothes had made her smile but she certainly wasn't thinking about them.

He watched her talk; he watched her as she replaced the receiver. He watched the quiet dignity as she thanked the nurse. He watched her walk back to him and he thought, she's a woman in a million. A woman to change your life plans for?

How crazy a thought was that?

'Our phone's back on,' she told him. 'It came back on just after we left. The line must be mended. Mickey's mum and dad are both there now and Jenny's stuffing our turkey and making brandy sauce. Millicent's calving hasn't progressed any further—Ian thinks the calf's a while off. The boys are playing with the cars. Jenny's called in the neighbours and three men are up on the roof putting tarpaulins over the capping in case there's rain before we can get a builder in. Oh, and they've fixed Santa Claus.'

'They've fixed…'

'But his sleigh's broken beyond repair. There's nothing they can do about that so Santa's escape route's gone. We're stuck with him.' She was smiling now, though her smile was a bit watery.

'Hooray,' he said faintly, and he couldn't keep his gaze from her face. Why hadn't he realised just how beautiful she was? He'd been blind.

'Hooray at last,' she repeated and her voice softened. 'It's all okay again. I have help. Scott says there's no rush to get home. Christmas is back on track. And…and it's thanks to you,' she said, and choked a bit again. 'You saved Letty. You saved us.'

'There's no need for hyperbole,' he said, embarrassed. 'You did some saving as well.'

'There's no way I would have got up on that roof in time to stop her falling.'

'You don't know what you can do until you must.'

'Indeed you don't,' she said, and her eyes were shining and she was close enough to touch. Close enough to…

She backed away, as if suddenly something had touched her, reminded her. 'I… that's all I wanted to say,' she faltered.

Was it all he wanted to say? He wanted more. He wanted to kiss her. In the middle of the emergency waiting room. With patients, medics, relatives everywhere.

He definitely wanted to kiss her.

'No,' she said, and he met her gaze with a jolt of shock. Of course. This woman was seriously good. She anticipated his needs. That was what he paid her for.

She'd anticipated this one and she was refusing.

'I… I don't think we need to stay here,' she managed. She glanced at her watch, and that tiny movement put more distance between them. It made what he wanted to do even more impossible. 'We should do something while we wait. Go down and look at the sea?'

'How about shopping?' he suggested. 'I checked yesterday—every shop in the city will be open today.'

'You're joking,' she said, startled. 'Walk through the Christmas crowds looking like this? We look like something out of *Chainsaw Massacre*.'

'Hence my shopping plan. Are you hungry?'

Her eyes widened at that, as if remembering something important.

'Yes,' she said. 'Yes, I am. Whatever happened to breakfast?'

He grinned. 'I guess it's still waiting beside the toaster at home.' *Home?* The word seemed to jar, and he corrected himself. 'Back at the farm.'

'We could grab a sandwich at the hospital cafeteria. I guess there is a hospital cafeteria.'

'I refuse to have hospital sandwiches on Christmas Eve. What I suggest…'

'Here we go.'

'What?'

'What you suggest…'

'What's wrong with that?'

'It's just *What I suggest* is McMaster for *What's going to happen*.'

'I'm open to discussion,' he said, wounded, and she was smiling again. More. She was laughing at him.

It was such a weird sensation that he felt winded.

No one laughed at him.

He kind of…liked it.

He grinned, and she grinned back, and suddenly there was such a frisson of tension between them that if a nurse hadn't approached he would have thrown reserve, caution, sense to the wind and taken her in his arms and kissed her, right on the spot. He still might…but the nurse was walking right up to them, speaking to Meg but glancing at him, as if he was included in this too.

Almost as if he was family.

'The stitching's done,' she said. 'The doctors used a very light general anaesthetic—they thought it was more appropriate, given how shocked she is—and we're popping in a little plasma to get her blood pressure up faster. I suspect she'll sleep for two hours at least. Can you give us that time before you take her home?'

'Yes,' William said before Meg could answer. 'Yes, we can.' He glanced at his cellphone and smiled. 'Hey, I have reception. I'll give you my number. Can you ring us when she wakes? Meanwhile, I suggest Miss Jardine and I find something decent to wear and then eat.'

'And if I want hospital sandwiches?' Meg muttered but she was smiling too.

'I'm your boss,' he said. 'That has to count for something.'

It counted for a lot, and so did money. Meg was simply led by William's 'suggestions'.

First, he took her to what the nurse had told him when he'd enquired was 'the classiest clothes shop in town'.

'She needs a frock,' William said to the bemused assistant. 'Or more. I suggest she buys three and everything that goes with them. Shoes, whatever.' He laid his credit card on the counter. 'Whatever it takes.'

'This feels like *Pretty Woman*,' Meg muttered. 'I'm not for sale.'

'I'm not buying.'

She met his gaze. Something passed between them, changed. *I'm not buying.*

Of course he wasn't, Meg thought. He had Elinor and women of her ilk. He escorted women from the pages of glamour magazines.

And, again, he knew what she was thinking. 'You're my PA,' he said, his tone softening. 'Nothing more. Don't get any ideas, Jardine. It's just that I don't like my PA in blood-spattered overalls.'

He sounded suddenly formal and she shivered. The warmth that had been growing inside, the comfort she'd felt as he'd held her, the bud of an idea, shrivelled.

The idea had been stupid—but she had to move on.

'And I don't like my boss in blood-spattered overalls,' she managed and tilted her chin.

'Which is why I'm heading to the place Scott showed me yesterday to buy even more jeans,' he said. 'So I'll leave you to it. No shaking while I'm gone. Everything's fine.'

And, before she could guess what he intended, he took her hands, tugged her towards him and kissed her lightly on the lips. Only it wasn't how she wanted to be kissed. It was back to where she'd started. It was a *Pretty Woman* kind of kiss. Take my plastic and buy what you need. I'll comfort you and care for you, because you're part of my entourage.

'Don't look like that, Miss Jardine,' he said softly. 'I'm not buying your soul. I'm only returning you to respectability.'

'Meg,' she said, and if she sounded forlorn she couldn't help it.

'I believe it should be Miss Jardine.'

'Willie,' she snapped and, before he could guess what she intended back, she grabbed his hands, tugged him toward her and kissed him as well. Harder. Defiant. 'Willie,' she said again and glowered.

His lips twitched. There was laughter behind his eyes. And admiration.

And something more?

Something quickly quelled. Something he didn't want to admit?

No matter, it was gone, he was gone, and she was left with his plastic.

'Wow,' the sales assistant breathed as he disappeared into the crowd of last minute Christmas shoppers. 'I wish my boy-friend would do something like this.'

'He's not my boyfriend.'

'Oh, but he's gorgeous.'

'In blood-stained overalls?'

'He'd be gorgeous in anything,' the girl breathed. 'Oh, miss… Oh, let's find you the prettiest dress in the shop. With a guy like that letting you use his credit card, you want to be gorgeous.'

'With a guy like that I should wear a faded bag over my head,' Meg muttered but the sales assistant was already haul-ing out offerings.

She should not accept his money. But…

I suggest…

This was W S McMaster talking. Her boss, giving orders. If she put things back on their rightful footing, she'd accept.

Miss Jardine would accept. It was only Meg who was having stupid quibbles.

'Show me what you have,' she said, resigned. Two more days of autocracy and he'd be gone. Or sooner. She should check the news on the air strike.

Why didn't she want to?

'What about this?' the sales assistant asked, and held up a dress that made her gasp. It was pretty in the real sense of the word. It was a nineteen-fifties halter neck, cinch-waisted frock with a full circled skirt. It was white with red dots. It was young, frivolous and so far away from what Meg always wore that she shook her head before she thought about it.

She wore sensible black skirts and white shirts, or she wore overalls, or she wore jeans, and somewhere at home she had a pale grey skirt for church and funerals.

She did not wear polka dots.

'Something sensible,' she said.

'It's Christmas,' the girl said and then she looked at Meg's overalls. 'And…excuse me for asking, but that looks bad.'

'It nearly was bad.'

'So it could have been bad,' the girl said and Meg realised she was in the hands of a master saleswoman. 'And, if it had been, you'd never have got the chance to wear polka dots. And he…' she looked meaningfully in the direction William had gone '…would never have seen you in polka dots.'

'Perish the thought,' Meg said, trying to sound sarcastic, but it didn't come off.

'So will you try it?'

No, Meg thought. But she couldn't say it.

She looked at the dress, and then she also glanced in the direction William had gone. She could no longer see him.

He'd be back.

Tomorrow or the next day he'd be gone.

What the heck. It was his plastic. *I suggest…*

She was merely following her boss's orders. Only he no longer felt like her boss. He felt like something else completely.

So did she. She stared into the mirror and saw the woman she'd been two days ago behind the woman she was now. And she thought of the impossibility of going back to what she had been.

I'll be one of those elderly secretaries, she thought, totally devoted to the boss, taking whatever he'll give. 'Good morning, Mr McMaster, of course I'll take dictation, certainly I'll send flowers to Sarah, I suggest tiger lilies because they're what the gossip columnists say is her favourite flower.'

Meanwhile...

Meanwhile, Scotty had climbed on the roof to put Santa up himself and Letty had tried to fix it. If she'd had a regular job, where she could go home every night...

She'd told herself this was better. Working twenty-four seven for short bursts and then staying home.

She'd loved twenty-four seven. She loved working for W S McMaster. But now...

Now she'd seen William clinging to the roof, holding her grandma. Now William had held her at the hospital and she'd needed him to hold her.

Two days ago she'd been able to draw a line—that life, this life.

The lines had blurred and it frightened her.

Decisiveness had always been her strong point. She didn't have to like it but she knew when a decision had to be made. She made one now. Oh, but it hurt.

She took a deep breath. She glanced once more in the direction William had gone. Before he came back, she had to find some resolution.

She took the polka dots and disappeared into the changing room...to change.

She was wearing polka dots.

He'd left her wearing bloodied overalls and truly disgusting boots. She was now wearing what could only be described as a happy dress, a Christmas dress. Her boots had been replaced with white strappy stilettos and her hair, caught back with an elastic band while she'd done the milking, was now a riot of bouncing curls, caught on the side with a tiny red rosette.

She looked about ten years younger.

She looked breathtakingly lovely.

Meg was gazing into the mirror as if she, too, hardly recognised herself. She met his reflected gaze and turned slowly to face him, and he thought if he hadn't caught her in this she might have fled and taken it off.

'It's…it's silly,' she said.

'It's lovely,' the shop assistant said definitely. 'We've found two more that are just as pretty, only she won't buy three. She's reluctant to buy even this one, but I persuaded her to try it on again. With shoes.'

'Well done,' he said, walking closer. 'I can see it needs shoes.'

'It's silly,' Meg said again.

'It's not,' William said, somehow managing to smile at the shop assistant without taking his eyes off Meg. 'You look lovely.'

She flushed. 'I feel like something out of Hollywood.'

'Great things come out of Hollywood. We'll take it.' He still hadn't taken his eyes from her. 'And the other two. Wrap the others. She'll leave this one on.'

'William…'

'Say "Yes, Mr. McMaster".'

'No!'

'You're intending to go to a classy restaurant wearing overalls?'

'I'm not going to any classy restaurant.' Her new resolution hadn't included socialising. She'd have a sandwich on the run and then go back to the hospital. Then she'd get through Christmas. She'd tell him her decision as she put him on the flight back to New York.

A withered spinster gazing adoringly after her boss… She hauled the conjured vision back into her head and held on to it.

Her decision was right, no matter how much it hurt. She had to move forward.

But he was still thinking restaurants. 'Of course we need to go to a restaurant,' he said, sounding wounded. 'I've bought new clothes too, so we're both dressed up. You like my chinos?'

He was smiling at her. Oh, that smile...

'They're fine, but...'

'Hey, I said you're lovely.'

'Okay, you're lovely too,' she muttered. 'But we don't need to match.'

'Better that we don't, I think,' he said softly. 'But we'll buy the dresses anyway.'

CHAPTER EIGHT

MEG walked out of the shop feeling as if she were in a freeze-frame from a fifties movie. William put his hand in the small of her back to guide her through the crush of shoppers and the feeling of unreality deepened.

'Don't think about it,' he said, obviously sensing how self-conscious she felt. 'The crowds were looking when you were covered in blood. They're still looking, but now they're smiling. Let's concentrate on the important things. Like breakfast.'

She'd given up fighting. A sandwich on the run felt good, but anything would do. She was so hungry she was likely to keel over. If he had to take her to a restaurant, then so be it.

'Yes, please,' she said, expecting him to take her into one of the small local restaurants. But instead he ushered her back into the car—how did this man manage to get a park when the whole world was looking for a park today?—and she almost groaned. She wanted to eat *now*.

But she'd worked for too long for this man to complain when meals took too long coming, so she stifled her groan and folded her hands in her lap and thought she looked ridiculous. She should be smiling and waving. But then they should be driving an expensive sports car instead of Letty's farm wagon. At least the silencer was fixed, she thought, and then she saw where they were going and she forgot about anything else.

He was driving up to the cliff above the town. He was taking her to the most expensive restaurant in the district.

She'd never been here.

'This place is… Oh, it's where you go to celebrate wedding anniversaries. When you're rich. They don't do breakfast,' she breathed.

'They do today. I rang them. I spoke to the chef personally. Bacon and eggs and fried bread and strawberries and fresh juice and sourdough toast and home-made butter… We had a long discussion. Anything we want, we can have.'

'If we pay.'

'If I pay,' he said gently and he was out of the car, striding round to her side and handing her out as if she was one of his dates instead of Miss Jardine, his PA.

He never handed her out of his car. He opened doors for her, the natural courtesy of a polite man, but to walk around and help her out of the car… no. She was his employee and the extra cosseting was reserved for…his women?

She no longer fitted either category, she thought, as she brushed past him and his touch made her feel even more as if this was not real, it was something out of a movie. The lines were blurring.

But if the lines were blurring… The question was huge and for some reason it was drumming in her head—insistent, urgent. There was never going to be a good time to ask—so why not now?

'Who's Elinor?' she asked, and he looked at her for a long moment and then smiled and shrugged and led her inside.

Maybe the lines were blurring for him too, she thought, and then she thought, all the more reason why her decision was the only possible one.

'I'll tell you over breakfast,' he said simply, and she knew she was right.

The restaurant was almost empty. This place started lunch

at what it deemed a respectable hour and this didn't quite qualify. Maybe they wouldn't have taken his booking if he hadn't…thrown his credit card around? Thrown his name around?

'You'll have the paparazzi in your face before you know it,' she said darkly and he shook his head.

'You think the paparazzi has nothing better to do on Christmas Eve than take photos of me? I'm low-key in the celebrity world.'

He was, she thought, but only because he created little stir. He didn't do the society thing. Even though his name was known worldwide, for the most part he deliberately kept away from cameras. He was seen in the celebrity magazines, stepping back into the shadows as his woman of the moment smiled and posed. If the women he escorted started to like the limelight too much, he moved on. Was this why she hadn't heard of Elinor until now? Did the woman have sense enough to stay low profile?

She shouldn't have asked. She had no business asking.

She really wanted to know.

The head waiter was leading them to what must surely be the best table in the house, in an alcove which gave a semblance of privacy but where the view stretched away across the ocean, as far as the eye could see. There were windsurfers on the waves below them. Meg thought suddenly, how long had it been since she'd swum?

Their farm was almost an hour's drive from the sea. There was never any time to indulge in anything so frivolous.

Maybe *when* she changed jobs…

The thought was inexorably bleak.

'Eggs and bacon and toast and fruit and juice and coffee,' William said to the waiter. 'Any way you want to serve them, as long as it starts coming fast. Is that okay with you, Miss Jardine?'

Miss Jardine. It sounded wrong. Maybe it sounded wrong to William too, because he was frowning.

'Yes. Wonderful,' she managed.

The waiter sailed off as if he'd just been given an order which was a triumph of creation all on its own—how much had William paid to get this table, to get a breakfast menu, to simply be here? To take his woman somewhere beautiful.

She was not his woman.

Neither was she Miss Jardine.

Deep breath. Just do it. 'Mr McMaster, this might not be the time to tell you, but I think I should,' she said and she faltered. Was she mad? Yes, she was. She knew it, but she still knew that she had no choice. 'I need to resign.'

William had glanced out to sea as a windsurfer wiped out in spectacular fashion. He turned back to face her and his expression had stilled.

'Resign?'

'I'll train my replacement,' she said hurriedly. 'I won't leave you without anyone. But you're going back to the States anyway. If you're gone for a couple for months I'll have someone sorted before you return. I'll work side by side with her then for a couple of weeks until I'm sure you're happy, but…'

'I hire my own PAs,' he snapped.

'So you do. Then, please, you need to find my replacement.'

'Can I ask why?'

There was the question. A thousand answers crowded in but he was watching her face—and this was William… No, this was W S McMaster…and she knew him and he knew her and only honesty would do.

'The work we do…we need to travel side by side. We need to be totally dependent on each other but we need to stay detached. Today… Up on the roof I got undetached.'

'Meaning?'

'Meaning I don't think of you as Mr McMaster any more. I think of you as the man who saved my grandma.'

His gaze didn't leave her face. 'So take a pay cut,' he said at last. 'I don't see how abandoning me is showing your gratitude.'

'You know what I mean.'

He did. She saw a flicker behind his eyes that might almost be read as pain if she didn't know how aloof this man was. How he stood apart.

'There's no need to leave.'

'I think there is.'

'You're under contract,' he snapped.

'No.' She met his gaze calmly, hoping he couldn't guess the tumult behind her words. 'My contract's up for renewal. It expires next month.'

'You're responsible for keeping contracts up to date.'

'So I am. So I have. My contract expires. It's not to be renewed, so we move on.'

'So you tell me now?' he snapped. 'And you expect us to calmly go on sharing Christmas when you no longer work for me?'

She flinched, but there was no avoiding what needed to be said. She knew him well enough now to accept the only way forward was honesty.

'It's the only way I can go on sharing Christmas,' she said simply. 'Feeling the way I do.'

'Feeling…'

'Like you're not my boss any more.'

'This is nonsense.'

'It's not nonsense,' she said stubbornly. 'I'm sorry but there it is. I've quit. If you want me to keep working until you get a replacement…'

'That means you'll still be working over Christmas.'

'I'm returning my Christmas bonus.' She glanced down at her dress. 'I'll take these in the form of severance pay. You won't be out of pocket.'

'What nonsense is this? You can't afford the grand gesture.'

'It's not a grand gesture,' she said stiffly. 'It's what I need to do. I can't afford not to.'

'What's that supposed to mean?'

'It means not everything's about money.' She hesitated. 'Who's Elinor?' she asked again and his brows snapped down in a sharp, dark line of anger.

'Is that what this is about?'

'You mean am I, your PA, jealous of a woman called Elinor?' She managed a smile at that one. 'Of course I'm not. All I'm saying is that the lines between personal and professional have been blurred. Last week I wouldn't have dared ask that question—I wouldn't want to. However, suddenly I want to know why you never had a dog when you were a kid. I want to know how you learned to climb when you were a boy. And, yes, I do want to know about Elinor.' She hesitated. 'Maybe this can't make sense to you, but a week ago I didn't mind…that you seemed aloof and a bit…unhappy.'

'I'm not unhappy,' he said, startled, and she thought about it.

'Okay, not unhappy,' she conceded. 'Wrong word, but I don't know what the word is. Just…holding yourself tight against the world, when letting the world in could make you happy.'

And he got it, just like that. 'Like caring about Scott and Letty?'

'Like caring about Scott and Letty.'

'And if anything happens to them?'

'Then my world falls apart.'

'Then that's dumb. You can't afford to think like that.'

'Why not? That's all there is.'

'Emotional nonsense.'

'So who's Elinor?'

'It's none of your business.'

'It's not,' she agreed. 'And as my boss you can tell me to mind my own. As a casual acquaintance you can tell me that as well. But now I'm your hostess for Christmas, and you saved my grandma's life. So I owe you and you owe me and I really want to know that there's someone in your life who can take that horrid, reserved look away from your face.'

He stared at her, nonplussed. She managed to meet his gaze and hold. This wasn't just about her, she thought. There was something she had to reach…something it was important to reach.

He'd saved Letty. She owed it to him to try.

But then breakfast arrived. The smell reached her before the meal, wafting across the room as a delicious, tantalising siren call. A couple of early lunch diners were being ushered to their tables. She saw their noses wrinkle with appreciation and she thought—mine, hands off.

She turned back to William, and the same thought flickered. *Mine…* Only it was a stupid, stupid thought. It was why she had to get out.

Maybe she didn't want to know who Elinor was. Personal or not, boss or…friend?…she didn't have the right.

But she wasn't retracting and her question hung.

And it seemed he'd decided to tell her. The meal was set before them and he started to talk even before he started to eat. There was anger beneath his words, an edge of darkness, but the words were coming out all the same.

'Elinor's a foster mother in Manhattan,' he said. 'She's a lovely, warm Afro-American lady with a heart bigger than Texas. She's old enough to retire but there are always children who need her. Right now she's fostering Ned and Pip.

Two years ago she took them in while their mother suppos-
edly undertook a court-ordered rehab, but instead she robbed
a drug store, with violence. She's been in prison ever since
and she doesn't contact them; she treats them with complete
indifference. Elinor's trying to persuade her to give them up
for adoption but she won't. So Elinor's the only mother they
know.'

'And...you?' she asked, stunned.

'I met Elinor when I agreed to sponsor the Manhattan
Foster-Friends programme. It's an organisation designed to
give foster carers support, for people who'd love to help but
who only have limited time to give. So Elinor and the children
have become my... Foster-Friends. I'd promised to take them
out for Christmas.'

'I see,' she whispered, and she did see. Sort of. So the
image of a sleek, sterile Manhattan apartment wasn't right.
Or maybe it was right; it was just that he moved out from it
in a way she hadn't expected.

'So what will they do now?' she asked, feeling dreadful—
for Elinor, for Pip and Ned, and for William himself.

'Elinor has said not to worry. She'll give them Christmas.
They don't depend on me.'

'Oh,' she said in a small voice.

'Eat your breakfast, Meg,' he said gently and she turned
her attention to her plate, though the enjoyment wasn't in it
now. Or not so much.

It did, indeed, look wonderful. Pleasure laced with guilt.

'I'm sorry I didn't get you home,' she said.

'It's not your fault. Eat.'

Eat. She'd almost forgotten she was hungry. Or maybe not.
She was fickle, she thought, piercing an egg and watching the
yolk ooze across the richly buttered toast. Mmm.

She glanced up and William was watching her and she
thought, with a tiny frisson of something she was far too

sensible to feel—*Elinor's a retirement age foster mother. And William cares about kids.*

But William only cared about these kids part-time. In the bits he had available. She knew he was out of the country eight months out of twelve.

The coldness settled back—the bleak certainty that this man walked alone and would walk alone for ever. There was nothing she could do about it. She'd resigned. She didn't have to watch him self-destruct.

But maybe he was right. Maybe he wasn't self-destructing—maybe it was she who was putting herself out there to be shot down with emotional pain.

The whole scenario was too hard. There was only one thing to do here.

She looked back down at her egg—firmly—and concentrated—firmly—on her truly excellent breakfast.

There wasn't a lot of conversation after that. After their third coffee William rang the hospital while Meg stared into the dregs of her cup. He put it onto speaker so Meg could hear the nurse's response.

'She's still asleep. Yes, she's fine. I promise we'll ring you the moment she wakes.'

'So let's walk,' he decreed and Meg could only agree. She didn't want to go back to the hospital and wait. And think.

Think of what she was walking away from.

So they walked down to the beach, and Meg slipped off her sandals and headed for the shallows.

William watched her from further up on the sand. He kept his shoes on. He'd swapped his boots for a pair of casual loafers but he wasn't taking the next step. W S McMaster with bare feet, walking in the shallows? Unthinkable.

She walked along, letting the last run of the waves lick over her toes, kicking sprays of water up in front of her.

William walked parallel to her but fifteen feet up the beach. She was in the shallows. He was on solid sand.

Solid sand?

There was no such thing, she thought. Nothing was solid. Everything was shifting.

Why wasn't he taking his shoes off? Why wasn't he coming close?

She knew why. She even agreed it was sensible that he shouldn't.

The wind was warm on her face. The sand and salt between her toes felt fabulous. All it needed was for William to take fifteen steps and take her hand and life would be...

A fairy tale.

So get real, she told herself and kicked up a spray of water so high she soaked the front of her dress. This guy is a billionaire from Manhattan—my ex-boss. I'm unemployed, with a hundred dairy cows, a little brother and a grandma who needs me and will need me for years.

She kicked the water again and glanced sideways at William.

He wasn't looking at her. He was striding along the beach as if he was there to walk off his too-big breakfast and that was that.

And why shouldn't it be that? The man hadn't been to the gym for two days. He'd be suffering from withdrawal.

'You go on by yourself,' she called to him. 'Burn some energy. I'm happy to stay here and kick water.'

He glanced at her and nodded, brisk, serious.

She turned to watch the windsurfers and he headed off along the beach. Alone.

He was being a bore.

He didn't know what else to be.

There were a thousand emotions crowding into his head right now and he didn't know what to do with any of them.

She was beautiful. There was a really big part of him that wanted to head into the shallows—with or without shoes—and tug her to him and hold.

How selfish would that be?

She wasn't like any woman he'd dated. He'd selected her with care as his Australian PA and that was what she was qualified to be. She was smart, efficient, unflappable. Loyal, honest, discreet. Sassy, funny, emotional.

Trusting and beautiful.

He didn't have a clue what to do with all these things. He moved in circles where women knew boundaries; indeed, they wanted them. He was an accessory, a guy with looks and money who was good for their image. No one had ever clung.

Meg wasn't clinging. The opposite—she was walking away.

That was good. She knew the boundaries. She knew they'd overstepped them so she was protecting herself. She had the right.

And if he stepped over the boundaries after her, like walking into the water now and taking her hand, pretending they could just be a normal couple, boy and girl...

He didn't do boy and girl. He had to leave; he knew no other way of living.

Do not depend on anyone.

He could depend on Meg.

No. She'd resigned. The thought hurt. He tried to drum up anger but it wasn't there. All that was left was a sense of emptiness, as if he'd missed out on something other people had. How to change? If he tried... If he hurt her...

He walked faster, striding along the hard sand, trying to drive away demons. He stopped and looked back, and Meg was a red and white splash of colour in the shallows, far behind.

In a day or two she'd be further away. She'd get some sort of hick job and be stuck here, milking her cows. Taking care of Letty and Scott.

It was her choice.

He picked up a heap of seaweed and hurled it out into the shallows, as if it'd personally done him injury. That was what this felt like, but he couldn't fault Meg. She was protecting herself, as he protected his own barriers.

She had the right.

He'd choose another PA and move on.

But first…he had to get Christmas over. Bring on Santa Claus, he thought grimly, followed by a plane out of here.

And then they'd all live happily ever after?

CHAPTER NINE

IT WAS a subdued trio who returned home. Letty was stretched out on the back seat, dozing. The doctors had been inclined to keep her; she'd woken enough to be stubborn but she was sleeping now.

Meg sat in the passenger seat, staring straight ahead. As if she was enduring something that had to be endured.

He'd made a few desultory attempts at conversation but had given up. So much for his smart, sassy PA. Now she was just…Meg. Someone he once knew?

Just concentrate on driving, he told himself. When he got back to the farm he'd move onto evening milking. The phone line was working again so after milking he could use the Internet; keep himself busy.

'By the way, I've organised your satellite connection,' he said and Meg cast him a glance that was almost scared.

'You what?'

'While you were dress shopping. It only took me minutes to buy what I needed, and the Internet place was open for business. It seems satellite dishes make great Christmas gifts. Even I couldn't get them to erect it today, but first working day after Christmas it'll be here.'

'I can't afford…'

'It's paid for. Three years in advance.'

'No, thank you,' she said in a tight, clipped voice. 'Three dresses are enough.'

But… 'Are you out of your mind?' Letty was suddenly awake, piping up from the back seat in indignation. 'Meg, what sort of gift horse are you looking in the mouth here? Scotty will love it. You know there'll be times still when he's stuck at home in pain. You can't say no to that.'

'Letty, I'm no longer working for Mr McMaster,' Meg said. 'So I can't take expensive gifts.'

'You're not working for him?'

'She's resigned. Tell her she's daft,' William said.

'No,' Letty said, surprisingly strongly. 'My Meg's not daft. If she's quit there's a good and sensible reason. But a satellite connection…that'd be a gift to Scotty and me, not to Meg, wouldn't it, Mr McMaster?'

'William,' he said and he almost snapped.

'William,' Letty said. 'Scott's friend. My friend. Meg, dear, William has more money than he knows what to do with, and he's just given us a very fine Christmas gift in return for a bed for Christmas. And…' She hesitated, but she was a wise old bird, was Letty. 'And you don't want anything in return, do you, Mr McMaster?'

'William!'

'William,' Letty said obediently. 'But you're not buying Meg with this. She doesn't owe you anything, right?'

'Right,' he said and glanced across at Meg. Her face was drawn, almost as if she was in pain.

He hated that look. He didn't know what to do about it.

'Then I accept on Scotty's behalf,' Letty said across his thoughts. 'And your bed for Christmas is assured.'

When they'd left the farm it had been almost deserted. When they turned back into the driveway there were more than a dozen vehicles parked under the row of gums out front.

'Uh-oh,' Letty said, peering dubiously out of the window. 'This looks like a funeral.'

'If it hadn't been for William, it would have been,' Meg said, and once again William thought she sounded strained to breaking point. 'If Scott's done something else stupid…'

But it seemed he hadn't. When they pulled up, women emerged from the house, men appeared from the yard, kids appeared from everywhere.

'They called a working bee,' Scott said, limping across to the car on his crutches and tugging open the back door to make sure for himself that his grandmother was in one piece. 'They said you had enough on your plate, Meg. And they knew you'd left the hay till after Christmas, so they brought slashers and they've done three whole paddocks. They're bringing in the last of it now.'

'You're kidding,' Meg whispered, but she was staring across to a hay shed which had stood almost empty this morning and now looked three-quarters full. 'In what—four hours?'

'We can work when we want to.' It was Jenny, coming forward to give her friend a hug. 'We were thinking we'd help after Christmas but when this happened I said to Ian, why not now?' She cast a curious glance at William. 'She needs looking after, our Meg.'

'I do not,' Meg said, revolted.

'She doesn't,' Scott said and Jenny grinned and hugged him as well until he turned scarlet in embarrassment.

'Okay, she doesn't. As long as you and Letty stop doing darn fool things when she's not around,' Jenny retorted.

'I'm going to be around,' Meg said. 'I'll try and find a job locally. I… I don't want to be away any more. But for now… thank you all so, so much. I'm incredibly grateful. But I need to get Letty inside. She needs to sleep.'

'I'll carry her,' William said but one of the neighbours

stepped forward and lifted Letty from the car before he could.

'We're local,' he said to William, quite kindly, but firmly for all that. 'We look after our own. Cows are on their way up now, Meg. You want some help with tonight's milking?'

'You've done enough,' Meg said.

'This guy'll help?' It seemed everyone was looking at William.

'He's promised to.'

'Is he any good?'

'At milking? He has untapped potential,' Meg said and people laughed and gathered their kids and said their goodbyes and left.

Meg tucked Letty into bed and fussed over her. Scott limped over to the cow yard and William followed.

'We should start,' Scott said.

William looked at the brace on Scott's leg and said gently, 'Is that okay? That you help with milking?'

'It has to be. I'm tired of waiting for it to heal.'

'So it's not okay.'

'Meg and Grandma fuss that if my leg gets kicked we have to start over again. But I'll be careful.'

'Or not. How about you supervise while I do the hands on?' William eyed the mass of cows pressing against the yard gate. He eyed the waiting bales. Nothing to this. Except… Maybe you had to do stuff to the vat for pasteurisation or… or something. He didn't want to waste a whole milking. 'Do you know how this works?'

'Course.'

'Then you give me instructions and leave me to it.'

'I can help.' Scott squared his shoulders. 'I know I was dumb trying to put that Santa up. I never dreamed Grandma'd try and fix it. But I'm not completely helpless. This leg'll soon be better. I can look after them.'

William looked into his drawn face. He saw reflected horror from this morning's accident. He saw the unmistakable traces of years of pain and he saw tension, worry, the pain of being a kid without a dad, an adolescent trying desperately to be an adult.

'I know you can,' he said softly. 'If you must. But I'm at a loose end right now, and it seems everything else is taken care of. So you sit on the fence and tell me your plans for your car restoration and in between plans you can tell me how to turn this milking machine on and let these girls get rid of their load.'

Scotty must be exhausted. Meg arrived at the dairy, back in her milking gear, and one glance at her little brother told her he was close to the edge. Physically, he was still frail. This morning would have terrified him and, with all the neighbours here helping, his pride wouldn't have let him stop.

She wanted to grab him down from the fence, hug him and haul him off to bed. But he was talking to William, who appeared to be underneath a cow, and she knew that pride still played a part here.

'So you two reckon you can run this place without me?' she enquired and William emerged from behind the cow and grinned.

'Nothing to this milking game. I'm about to add Milker to my CV.'

'How is he, Scotty?' she asked and then corrected herself. 'Sorry, Scott.'

'You can still call me Scotty if you like,' her brother conceded. 'In private.'

'In front of William's not private.'

'No, but he's okay.'

That was a huge concession, Meg thought. There'd been

a few guys in her past—of course there had—but Scott had bristled at all of them. *He's okay.* Huge.

'Just because he bought you bits of cars…' she managed, feeling choked up.

'No, he really is okay. Is Grandma asleep?'

'Almost,' she said and here was a way to let him off the hook without injuring any more of that fragile manly ego. 'She wants to say goodnight to you. Do you reckon you could stay with her while we milk? I'm still a bit worried about her.'

'Sure,' Scott said and slid off the fence and again she had to haul herself back from rushing forward to help. 'Watch William with those cups, though. Four teats, four cups. It's taking him a bit of time to figure it out.'

'Hey!' William said, sounding wounded, and Meg laughed and watched her little brother retreat and thought this was as good as it got.

But it was so fleeting. Tomorrow or the next day, William would be gone.

It was okay. This was the right thing to do. She had no choice but to resign. A PA, hopelessly devoted to her boss? That was pathetic and she knew it.

She glanced at him and thought, dumb or not, she was hopelessly devoted. She had no choice but to get as far from William as possible.

'He's a great kid,' William said and she flushed and started milking and didn't answer.

'You don't agree?' he asked after she'd cupped her first cow.

'Of course I agree.'

'But you're not talking.'

'It's been a big day.'

'But it's normal again now,' he said gently. 'Though it's a shame you felt the need to change. I liked your dress.'

'I'll wear it again tomorrow.' She gathered her emotions

and told them firmly to behave. Two days max and he'd be gone. 'Tell me about Pip and Ned. Do you have Christmas gifts for them?'

'I do.'

'What?'

'Bubble guns,' he said. 'Battery powered. Ten bubbles a second and they're seriously big.'

'You sound like you tried them out.'

'Why wouldn't I?'

Whoa… The thought of W S McMaster with a bubble gun… 'Whereabouts did you try them out?'

'On my balcony. I sent bubbles over Central Park.'

She giggled. Then she remembered he was going home and she stopped giggling.

'Meg?' he said softly from behind a cow.

'Yes?'

'Reconsider.'

'Quitting?'

'Yes.'

'No.'

'Why not?'

'Not negotiable,' she said. 'Being your assistant means being aloof.'

'You were never aloof.'

'I was aloof in my head.'

'And you're not now?'

'No,' she said shortly. 'Can we keep on milking?'

'Of course we can. As long as you keep on thinking about reconsidering.'

'I can't.'

'Don't think can't. Think of all the reasons why you just might can.'

'That's a crazy thing to say.'

'Resigning's a crazy thing to think.'

* * *

Only of course she was right and it was non-negotiable. They both knew it.

They finished milking, they cleaned the yard, they worked in tandem and mostly they worked in silence. Then they headed inside and ate the last of the trifle and bread and ham in that order because Letty and Scott were both deeply asleep and it didn't seem to matter what order they ate in.

William thought back to Christmas Eve meals he'd had as a child. Christmas had been an excuse for socializing, which meant huge parties of very drunk people. Because it was Christmas his parents had insisted he be part of it. At Christmas they had to pretend to be a family.

Here…for the past two days they'd lived on Letty's vast trifle and chunks of the huge Christmas ham and fresh bread and butter, eating as they felt like it, and it had felt… okay. Sensible. Delicious, even. But not…right?

The world seemed out of kilter somehow, William thought as he washed the dinner dishes and Meg wiped beside him. It felt so domestic, and domestic was something he'd never felt. Doing the washing-up with his PA was weird. All of today had been weird.

He'd lost his PA.

He'd lost Meg.

'We have the Internet back on,' Meg said as she put away the last plate. 'There's a phone connection in the attic—I use the attic as an office when it's not a spare bedroom—so you can catch up on the outside world before you go to sleep.'

'And you?'

'I'm checking on Millicent and then I'm going to bed. Christmas or not, it's still a five a.m. start. Goodnight, William.'

'Do you want help with Millicent?'

'She's not looking much different to this morning. I doubt if anything's happening tonight. Goodnight,' she said again, and she took the torch and headed out through the back door. The day was ended.

He'd check the Internet. He'd see what was happening with air traffic. He hadn't even checked today; maybe it was resolved.

Maybe he could leave.

Meg had already left.

Maybe things *were* happening tonight. She'd started again. Millicent was back to being uncomfortable, or more than uncomfortable, Meg thought. Her tail was constantly high, her back was arched and her eyes told Meg that she was in pain.

'Hey, it's okay,' Meg told her, fondling her behind the ears, scratching her, letting her rub her big head against her chest. This cow had been raised as a pet. She was a big sook and Letty loved her.

A normal dairy farmer would go to bed now, set the alarm and check her in a couple of hours. But, when she stepped back, Millicent's eyes widened in fear. Meg sighed and went back to the house and fetched a folding chair, a lantern, a book and a rug.

'Happy Christmas,' she told Millicent as she settled down to wait. 'You and me and hopefully a baby for Christmas. We should do this in a manger. Or, at the very least, at the bottom of the haystack.'

But Millicent wasn't going anywhere. Trying to move her now would only add to her distress and the night was warm enough.

'Who needs a manger, anyway?' Meg muttered and glanced upward to where a thousand stars glittered in the clear night sky. 'This is where babies should be born. So get on with it.'

Millicent rolled her eyes.

'I know, sweetheart, it's hard,' Meg said. 'Or I don't actually know. I've heard it's hard. You should have its daddy holding your hoof.'

She was being ridiculous.

She was thinking of William. The book she'd brought out to read was a romance. She and William. Having a baby. William coaching her through...

'Well, pigs might fly,' she muttered and tossed her romance aside and snuggled under her blanket. 'We're two single ladies, Millicent, and we need to get on with it together. You do your bit and I'll do mine.'

There'd been a last minute offer to the air traffic controllers. The union officials had deemed it worth considering and had sent out urgent contact to its members. Because this was Christmas they'd vote online. If enough members voted by midnight, planes could start flying as soon as tomorrow morning.

Great. He might get home almost by Christmas, he thought. He'd gain a day flying from Australia to the States. If he left on Christmas Day, then he'd arrive on Christmas Day.

He could give Ned and Pip their gifts. He could see them again; take them out to dinner, maybe.

Leaving Meg?

She was his employee. His ex-employee. So what was the problem leaving her?

No problem at all.

He intended to help with milking at five. He needed to go to sleep.

He lay in bed and stared at the ceiling and thought of...

Meg.

He thought of Meg for a long time. He tried to think of anything but Meg but she was superimposed, like a veil through which he saw everything else.

Or maybe…maybe everything in his life was a veil and Meg was behind. The only substantial thing.

What sort of crazy thinking was this? Where was the logic? Furious with himself, he threw off his covers and paced over to the attic window.

Two o'clock. The stars were amazing.

There was a light in the paddock beside the dairy. A faint light from a lantern. Someone was beside it.

Millicent? Was she calving?

Meg would be down there, making sure things were okay.

What business was it of his? He didn't know the first thing about birthing calves. He'd be no help at all.

But, now he knew she was there, doing nothing was impossible. He'd help if he could, he thought grimly, and then he'd leave.

He tugged on his overalls and headed downstairs.

What sort of life was this? Meg had been awake since five this morning. She'd be asleep on her feet, he thought as he made his way across the yard towards the lantern, but then he thought of all the times he'd demanded she stay up late, that she be awake for an early flight, that she continue until the work was done.

That was different. She was Miss Jardine then. He paid her to work when he worked.

He had three PAs. He thought of them now, and thought how hard did he work them? They never complained.

He paid them not to complain.

But, for the first time, he felt a niggle of guilt. He treated his employees fairly; he made it clear at the outset what he expected and he paid well. He had a loyal and long-serving staff because of it. But his demand that they stay impersonal…

His PAs told him what he needed to know about his staff. But his PAs themselves… Miss Darling, Mrs Abraham, Miss

O'Connell? He'd have to look up their staff profiles to find out what their family background was.

What was happening to him? His staff were turning into people. And you got attached to people. *Do not get attached to people you pay.*

Meg was messing with his head, that was what it was. The sooner he was out of here, the better.

Only she was in trouble. As he neared, he could see...

Millicent was down, flat on her side, her body arched and her neck stretched up as if straining to the limit.

Meg...yes, it was Meg...was lying behind her, a dark shadow behind the light. He could see a mat laid out to the side, a couple of buckets, rags, ropes...

'Problem?' he asked as he came up beside her and she didn't react. He looked more closely—and discovered why she didn't react. She was hardly in a position to concentrate on anything but the cow.

What was she doing?

'What's happening?' he asked, squatting beside her.

'Dystocia,' she said, gasping. 'I can't.'

She was lying flat, hard against Millicent's rear. Her arm...

'Dystocia?'

'Birth problems.' She sounded as if she'd been running. 'First calf. Bull was too big and now this. I knew it. I can't...'

'What can't you do?' he said, feeling helpless. He'd never seen a birth. He never wanted to see a birth.

Obviously, he was going to see this one.

Or more than see. 'Maybe you can help,' she gasped, and he thought maybe he should head back to his nice safe attic right now. Only a coward would run.

He surely felt like a coward.

'You're stronger than I am,' she gasped and he thought, uh oh.

'Can we call the vet?'

'He's away until after Christmas. He warned us.'

'Surely there's more than one vet.' He was taking in the whole scene now and, as he did, Millicent strained. Her whole body heaved and Meg moaned, and moaned again.

'What are you doing?'

'I can't...' She gasped, not able to continue until the contractions subsided. Then... 'Yes, we need a vet but we only have one locally. And the calf's leg's tucked backward instead of forward, meaning there's a ridge of shoulder stopping the birth. So I need to get the head back in the birth canal so there's room to turn it. But I can't. I don't have the strength.' She pushed and pushed again—and then seemed to make a decision. Her arm was suddenly free. She dunked it in the nearest bucket and looked up to him. 'Can you?'

'Can I what?'

'Push the head back far enough so you can get the leg forward.'

He felt as if someone had punched him. Milking was one thing, but this? 'You want me to...'

'I'm not strong enough,' she said simply. 'Please.'

'You think I...'

She wasn't listening. 'Rip your shirt off—it'll be ruined. Shove your arm into the disinfectant and I'll lubricate it. Hurry, before the next contraction.'

'You want me to...'

'Just do it,' she snapped and he was hauling his shirt off, thinking...thinking...nothing.

He dunked his arm in disinfectant. Meg wiped it and then started lathering him with some sort of jelly. He felt too winded to object.

'Lie flat,' she told him. 'If a contraction hits, don't try to do anything except stop the head coming further forward. But the foreleg on the right is lying back instead of hoof-forward. You need to push the head back far enough so you have space to feel the foreleg and tug it forward. There's no way she can get the calf out with it back.'

'I have no idea how to do that.'

'Simple,' she snapped. 'Cows have two forelegs. To calf they both need to be forward with the head between. So you pull a leg forward.'

'How do I know what everything is?'

She wasn't listening to his panic. She was intent only on instructions. 'It's not brain surgery. A hoof's easy to feel. Think about it. Think what you're looking for and then find it. Gentle as you can—do no damage—but you have to move fast. Before the next contraction. Go.'

So he lay full length on the grass and he did the unthinkable. To his astonishment, he could feel... What? He could feel the head. He could feel one small hoof on the left.

He needed the matching one.

Another contraction rippled through and he discovered why Meg had moaned. He almost moaned himself.

'Don't try and do anything during the contraction. Just hold it,' she snapped from above him and he held with all the strength he had and he knew that if he hadn't been holding the head would be emerging.

With one hoof and not the other.

So he held and finally, blessedly, the contraction eased.

'Now push,' Meg said urgently. 'All the force you can. You need to get it back.'

He didn't need to be told. He pushed, gently at first and then, as his grip tightened, as he became more sure of what he was holding, he pushed with more force. Then he pushed with all his strength.

The head moved...and then more...

'Now.' Meg would have seen by his arm that the head had shifted. 'Before the next contraction. Find the leg.'

He had to loosen his grip on the head, slide his fingers to the side… It was so tight….

But there it was, a bony joint, surely the leg. He felt along it, conscious of the need for speed…

He had it, hooked by two fingers, and he was tugging it forward.

'Careful not to rip anything,' Meg said urgently. 'Take care.'

Another contraction. He felt it coming, released the leg, held the head. Just held.

Then, as the contraction eased, he moved again, only this time he knew what he was looking for.

He had it. He pulled, hard, hoping he wasn't doing more harm than good, but the limb was slithering round, shifting, and there seemed to be room…

He had it!

'It's round,' he muttered and Meg's hand was on his shoulder, pressing him in a move of exultation. She was lying against him, full length on the dirt.

'Aligned?'

He knew what she meant and he could feel it. He had two neat hooves with the head between.

'Yes. Here's another….'

'Let it come,' she said. 'It'll come now.'

And it did, the next contraction shoving everything forward. Two hooves were out, and Meg was fastening them before the head appeared, tying them carefully with some sort of soft rope.

'What…'

'Just in case we need to help her,' she said. 'She's been straining for too long already and this calf is big. I'll loop this above and below the fetlock so we can pull without doing damage.'

'Where did you learn to do this?' he demanded, dazed, and he felt her smile rather than saw it.

'You mean why wasn't it on my CV? I can't think why I didn't include it. Here we go.'

Another contraction. Meg let it pass but the head didn't emerge.

'Okay, let's give her a hand,' she said. 'Can you take the rope? Tug with the contraction, not too hard, not enough to hurt the calf, I'm happy with an inch or two at a time.'

He nodded. Meg's hands were lubricated again. She was feeling…

'Now,' she said and he tugged.

A little further.

'Man, this head's big,' Meg said. 'With the size of this brain, you must be having the smartest baby on the planet, Millicent. He'll take a lot of knitting for a baby bonnet.'

Her voice was low and even and, with a sense of shock, William realised that, even though most of Meg's attention was on the calf, there was solid affection and worry for the cow as well.

She'd given her heart to a cow? How nuts was that? Where was his clinically efficient, unemotional PA now?

Gone. And the sense of loss was gut-wrenching.

'Now,' she said again, and then moaned because her hand was cupping the head, shoehorning it, and William was tugging on the hooves and there was only so much room…

'Keep going,' she managed as the contraction lengthened and he tugged some more, slowly, insistently and suddenly the head was there, the rope was no longer needed, the calf was half out.

Millicent gave a long bovine moan and Meg cleared membrane from the tiny nose and then laid her hand on Millicent's flank.

'Nearly there, girl. One more push. You can do it.'

One more contraction and the thing was done. The calf slithered out into the lantern light, a long wet bundle of spindly legs and black nose and rag-like tail. Meg cried out in delight and checked its nose was still clear and then lifted it around a little so Millicent could reach her baby with ease.

And she did. She turned and nosed her baby and she started to lick it clean. And William looked at Meg and saw her eyes were filled with tears and a man would have to be inhuman not to be moved. Not to take her into his arms…

Millicent had taken over, licking her calf with solid maternal ownership. Meg shifted away and her body collided with William's—and she didn't move any further.

He'd slipped the loop from the calf's hooves. He'd done all he could. Meg had done all she could. Their calf was alive and well—and Meg was hard against him.

He'd helped birth a calf. He and Meg. The feeling was awesome.

They were still half lying on the ground, and Meg was warm and beautiful, stained, filthy, her face tracked with tears…

She was trembling, her body reacting to the combined terrors of this day. How could he bear her trembling? How could he bear not to put his arms round her and tug her closer? So he did and, as he felt her yield, he tugged her closer still. Her hair brushed his face and he kissed the top of her head, just lightly, no pressure, nothing.

The awe from the birth was all around them—the stars, the warmth of the night, the feeling that a miracle had happened. New life… Did she feel this every time she delivered a calf? he wondered, but then he forgot to think more because she was turning in his arms and she was looking straight at him, her eyes huge and shadowed, vaguely troubled, but nevertheless…sure.

Sure that he'd kiss her. Sure that she wanted him to kiss her. He knew it and it was one more thing to add to the glory of this night—or maybe the whole night had been building to this kiss.

Maybe his whole life had been building to this kiss.

That was a crazy thing to think—but how could he think it was crazy when his hands were cupping her face and he was drawing her in to meet him? How could he think he was crazy when his mouth was lowering to hers and she was so sweet, so beautiful, so right?

She melted in to him, her mouth seeking his, her hands taking his shoulders so she could centre herself, be centred. Her need was as great as his. He could feel it in the urgency of her hold, in the fire he felt the moment he found her mouth.

She wanted him. He felt her need and his whole body responded. Their kiss was suddenly urgent, hard, demanding. It was as if a magnetic field had been created, locking them to each other, two force fields meeting as they must, with fire at the centre.

He wanted her. He wanted her fiercely, with a passion that rocked him. He felt…out of control.

Maybe he was out of control. It was Christmas Eve. He was in the centre of a paddock somewhere in Australia—he didn't truly know where—with a woman he'd thought he knew but he now realised he hadn't known at all.

His Meg.

No. Just Meg. Her own beautiful self.

He deepened the kiss and she responded with heat and need, her lips opening, her tongue searching. Oh, but he wanted her… His hands were on her breasts, but she was wearing overalls. How did you get through overalls?

She was buttoned to the throat. No. Not buttons. Studs.

They unfastened with satisfactory pops. Underneath the overalls was a lacy bra, and underneath the bra… His breath drew
in, with awe and wonder.

His hands were cupping her, and he'd never felt such beauty.
He'd never wanted a woman so much as he wanted Meg right
now.

No woman before had been Meg.

He rolled back with her and she came, smiling down into
his eyes. They were lying full length, wanting each other with
a desperate heat they could read in each other's eyes.

She was above him, smiling in the moonlight. Meg, his
beauty. Her skin was pale and luminous, she almost seemed
to shine.

They were on a horse rug or somesuch, something she'd
spread in the middle of a cow paddock. No pillowed bed could
feel better. No bed could feel more right.

'You're not taking your overalls off,' she whispered and he
realised with a shock that she was laughing. 'Not fair.'

His overalls were all in one. He'd pulled them on in a rush.
Underneath… Well, there wouldn't be a lot of finesse in his
undressing.

'You're wearing a bra,' he managed. 'I don't believe I'm
wearing anything.'

Her chuckle was so sexy it took his breath away. 'I think
that's good.'

'You don't want me out of my overalls,' he said but he
couldn't say it with any degree of certainty. This night…any-
thing was possible this night.

'And if I do?'

There was a statement to take his breath away. But a man
had to have sense, even if finding it almost tore him in two.
'I'm not…' Hell, it was so hard to get his voice to work. 'I'm
not carrying condoms.'

She paused at that. She stilled. He kissed her again, a

gentle, wondrous exploration that left him wanting more. Much more.

Why hadn't he thought of condoms? Of all the stupid… He didn't even have them in his bag back at the house.

He'd hardly packed thinking he was about to seduce his PA.

And Meg was tugging away, propping herself up on her arms, considering him in the dim light. 'How big's your head?' she asked and he blinked.

'Pardon?'

'Millicent operated with no condoms,' she said, her voice husky and shaken. 'Look what happened to her.'

He laughed, but it was a shaken laugh. He pulled away a little, sense returning. A little.

'We can't,' he managed. 'Unless Santa arrives right now.'

'I didn't put condoms on my Santa list,' she whispered, her voice laced with a thousand regrets.

'That's not efficient of you.'

'I'm not feeling efficient.'

'You don't look efficient,' he said and he tugged her to him again and held. He just held. 'My obstetrician extraordinaire.'

'Hey, you turned the leg. Maybe you've found your new calling.'

'I'm not ready for a new career. If it's all the same to you, I think I'll stick to the old one,' he said. But, the moment he said it, he knew it was a mistake.

Or maybe it wasn't a mistake. Maybe it was simply the truth, which had to be put out there.

It had killed the moment. Meg moved back, squatted back on her heels and looked at him for a long moment, as if searching his face. And, whatever she was looking for, she didn't find it. She smiled again, a wry little smile with all the regret in the world, and she tugged her overalls up to decency.

'Well, that was fun,' she said and suddenly he had Miss Jardine back—clinical, cool, ready to move on. 'Birth does crazy things to your head. Imagine how I'd feel if ever I was around a human birth. Lucky I'm not. But enough. It's three hours till milking. I need some sleep.'

'Meg...'

'No,' she said.

'No?'

'No.' She met his gaze, calm and cool in the moonlight, and if there was bleakness behind it there wasn't anything he could do about it. 'This was moon madness. We both know it, and it bears out my decision that I need to quit. What if there'd been a condom round tonight? We'd have been lost.'

Lost. The word hung between them, loaded with too many meanings.

'Will you help me pack up?' she said. 'Millicent will be fine for what's left of the night. It's lovely and warm. She has a fine heifer calf to clean and she'll do it better without us.'

'Heifer?'

'A little girl. I think we'll call her Milly. Millicent, mother of Milly. It has a fine ring to it, don't you think?'

She was talking for the sake of talking, he realised. She was putting emotion aside.

'I don't want to leave you,' he said simply and she looked at him for a long moment, considering, and then she shook her head.

'You can't take me with you. I don't fit. I did when my role was PA. No more. Somehow we've messed this and all there is now is for us to get on with our lives. You've got Ned and Pip and Elinor waiting for you back in New York, and you have your life there. I have a grandma and a little brother, and dairy cows and dogs and one brand new calf. That's enough to keep any girl happy.'

'Is it?'

'Yes,' she said, rising and dumping ropes into buckets. 'Yes, it is. Yes, it must be.'

CHAPTER TEN

WILLIAM woke to an operatic soprano belting out *Silent Night* right underneath his attic. Letty was singing along, almost louder than the soprano. A couple of dogs were joining right in.

Five-thirty. He'd been in bed for what—two and a half hours—and he'd lain awake for at least one of them.

He groaned and put his pillow over his head and then Scotty started singing too, and more dogs joined in, full howl.

Christmas. Hooray.

Feeling more like Scrooge every minute, he hauled his jeans on and staggered downstairs. The kitchen table was groaning with food in various states of preparation. Letty was wearing a truly astonishing crimson robe and a Santa hat. Scotty was sitting in his pyjamas, shelling peas. The difference between now and yesterday was astonishing.

'Happy Christmas,' Letty said, beaming. 'Great pecs.' Then, as he tried to figure whether to blush, she motioned to the sound system in the corner where, mercifully, *Silent Night* had just come to an end. 'My favourite carol. You want us to play it again?'

'She'll make you sing,' Scotty warned and William looked at the pair of them and saw exactly why Meg loved them to bits. A blushing adolescent and an old lady with her arm bandaged to her elbow, a lady who had almost died yesterday, who was now stirring something vaguely alcoholic, or possibly more than vaguely.

'Eggnog,' Letty said, following his gaze. 'Just on finished. You want first glass?'

'At five-thirty in the morning?'

'Yeah, it's late,' Letty said. 'Meg's already milking, without her eggnog. You want to take some over to her?'

'No,' he said, revolted.

'What's wrong with my eggnog?'

'If I'm going to help her milk, I need to be able to count teats.'

'He has trouble getting to four, Grandma,' Scotty said kindly. 'We'd better let him off eggnog till the girls are milked.' He hesitated. 'You will help milk, won't you? Meg said you helped so much last night that she wouldn't wake you, but she'll be ages alone.'

'I could help,' Letty said darkly. 'Only she won't let me.'

'With your arm? You're as dodgy as I am,' Scott retorted and once again William was hit with the sensation that he was on the outside, looking in. Family?

'Okay, toast and coffee and no eggnog until afterwards, but there's home-made raspberry jam,' Letty told him, moving right on. 'And real butter. None of that cholesterol-reducing muck this morning.'

'Grandma...' Scott said and Letty grimaced and held up her hands in surrender.

'I know. Back to being good tomorrow. You needn't worry, young man; I intend to be around to boss you for a long time to come.'

'So no more Santa rescues.'

'I'll be good,' she said and William saw a flash of remembered terror from yesterday and he thought she wasn't as tough as she was making out. She was brave, though. And he saw

Scott worrying about her and he thought that courage came in all guises.

They were all brave. And Meg… What she'd been trying to do for all of them since her parents' death…

'So you know about Millicent's calf,' he ventured, feeling really off centre, and they both grinned, happiness returning.

'Of course we do,' Scott said. 'She's gorgeous. And Meg said you got a backward hoof out. I wish she'd called me. I could've have helped.'

'There'll be lots of calves for you to help in the future,' Letty said roundly. 'We'll get *your* leg right first. We're just lucky William was able to help. We're very pleased to have you here,' she said to William. 'Now, Meg checked the news before she milked and she says the planes are running again. She and Scott checked flights and there are some available. She said to tell you when you woke up. But you don't want to leave yet, do you?'

'I…'

Did he want to leave? They were looking at him expectantly. Over in the dairy, Meg was milking, alone.

His world was twisting, as if it was trying to turn him in a direction he hadn't a clue about.

'I do need to go,' he said at last and it was as if the words were dragged out of him. 'If I help with the milking now, Scott, would you mind making me a list of flights and times?'

'*Today?*'

'Yes, please.'

'You really want to leave?' Scott demanded incredulously, and William thought about last night, thought about holding Meg. Thought about holding Meg again.

If he got any closer…

If Letty had fallen yesterday… If Scotty had been killed in that accident…

If anything happened to Meg...

Do not get close. Do not open yourself to that sort of pain.

'I don't want to go,' he said, striving not to let his voice sound heavy. 'How could I want to leave Letty's eggnog? But I do need to get back to Manhattan as soon as possible. So please let me know which flight might be available.'

'Okay,' Scotty said and, even if the kid did sound disappointed, William couldn't let that stand in the way of a decision that must be made.

He headed back upstairs to dress and, as he did, Letty adjusted the sound system. Next on the playlist was *Deck the Halls* and she turned the sound up even louder.

This place was crazy.

Of course he had to get out of here.

Meg was milking, head down behind a cow. When he reached the yard she didn't emerge, just kept on doing what she was doing. Killer and the rest of the dog pack greeted him with pleasure but there wasn't a lot of pleasure emanating from Meg.

That had to be okay by him. Maybe it was even sensible. He ushered the next cow into a bale and started doing what had to be done. He was getting good at this. Where could he use this new skill when he left?

Would he ever milk a cow again?

'Happy Christmas,' Meg said at last from behind her cow and he thought she sounded exhausted. Had she slept at all?

He wanted to tell her to go back to bed, that he'd take over. He couldn't. Yes, he'd learned new skills but he couldn't milk by himself yet.

If he left today... Would she be milking the cows alone?

'Happy Christmas,' he replied at last. Cautiously.

'The airlines are back. I'm sorry but I didn't have time to check flights before milking.'

'Not good enough,' he growled, trying for a smile, but she stiffened and said nothing.

'I was joking.'

'I know.'

'I'm sorry,' he said. 'Bad joke.'

'I'm sorry too,' she said, straightening and heading out to fetch another cow in. 'Last night...it should never have happened. It was like... I'd been so worried. It was reaction; nothing more.'

'It felt like more.'

'Well, it wasn't,' she snapped. 'Fortunately, the airlines are operating. We'll see if we can get you a flight out tonight.'

'What about milking?'

'What about milking?'

'Who's going to do it?'

'I will,' she said. 'I've done it alone plenty of times before. It just takes longer.'

'You're exhausted already.'

'Kerrie's back tomorrow—she's coming for lunch today so maybe she can even help tonight—and I can sleep in the middle of the day.'

'And then you need to job hunt.'

'I believe I'm still employed by you until my contract expires.'

'So you are.'

'So I'll keep the office operating here as my contract specifies. That'll give me time to find something else.'

They were being absurdly formal, he thought, but maybe formal was the only thing to be.

'What sort of job do you want?' he asked.

'I'm a qualified accountant.'

'You'll do accountancy in a provincial city?'

'What's wrong with that?'

'What a waste.'

She didn't bother responding. She just kept right on milking.

'You don't need to keep the office operating,' he said at last.

'You can't dismiss me without notice.'

'I'm not dismissing you. I'll pay you till the end of your contract.'

'Then I'll work till the end of my contract. I've taken enough from you. I can't take any more.'

'I'd like to give more.'

'Like what?' she said from behind her cow and he thought about it. What would he like to give her?

Money. Security. The knowledge that she wouldn't have to get up to milk a cow unless she wanted to.

The ability to drop everything and be with Scott when and if he needed further operations. The ability to care for Letty as she needed to be cared for. Financial freedom to call the vet whenever she needed the vet.

Freedom to have a bit of fun.

But this was nothing he could do. He'd given Scott his old cars. He'd given Meg dresses and he'd given them all the satellite dish. He knew without asking that she'd accept nothing else.

So there was nothing more he could do. There was nothing more he should do. As soon as his flight was confirmed, he could walk away and not look back.

That was what he wanted, wasn't it? Anything else was way too complicated.

Dogs. Cows.

Family.

'We'd best get a move on,' she said across his thoughts.

'We don't do Santa until the cows are done and then there's church and then there's eggnog.'

'You don't do eggnog until after Santa and church?'

'Not very much,' she said and managed a smile. 'Grandma doesn't tip up the brandy bottle until we're all safe home.'

Milking finished, William swished the dairy while Meg went to check on Millicent and the brand new Milly. They were standing contentedly in the home paddock, Milly at her mother's teat, no sign of the trauma associated with her birth.

If she was a hard-headed businesswoman, she'd remove the calf now, Meg thought ruefully as she looked down at the pretty little calf. After the first few hours, when the calf had taken the all important colostrum, efficient dairy practice was to remove the calf and get the cow straight into mass production.

Only neither Letty nor Meg were hard-headed. The calves stayed with their mothers until Letty decreed they were ready to be independent, which lost them milk production but probably made them a healthier herd. Or possibly made them a healthier herd. Or not.

It was a decision of the heart, not of the head.

'Like me stopping working for William,' she told Millicent and sat on the edge of the trough while she watched the cow and her new little calf. Killer nosed up beside her and shoved his head against her ribs. She hugged him tight and suddenly she felt like crying.

'And that's also dumb,' she told Killer. 'Why cry? For that matter, why quit? Working for the McMaster empire's the best job I've ever had. Why can't I keep on doing it? Why can't I ignore how I feel about him and get on with it?'

She knew she couldn't.

He was watching her. He was sluicing the yard but she could feel his gaze. She hugged her dog hard, then straightened her shoulders and rose and tried to look professional, as if she was examining cow and calf as a proper dairy farmer should. In terms of what she could make from them.

Millicent's eyes were huge and contented and maybe a little bit wondrous. While Meg watched, she started to lick her calf and the little calf kept right on feeding.

Drat, those tears kept right on welling.

'Happy Christmas, you great sook,' she told herself angrily and swiped at her cheeks with venom. 'Get a grip. And stop crying right now.'

She had to stop crying. William was finished in the yard. She should wait for him and walk him back to the house.

He was helping her. It'd be only civil to walk back.

But the feeling of that kiss of the night before was too huge, too raw, too real. It was threatening to overwhelm her.

'If I head back now I get first shower,' she told Killer. 'That's what a hard-headed, professional dairy farmer should do. And that's what I am.'

Right.

'Go fast before he catches up.'

Even more right. Or not.

He'd never seen a Christmas tree like it.

They'd been so busy, William had hardly been in the sitting room until now, but after a second breakfast and a little eggnog—yes, the serious stuff would come after church—Letty bossed them into the sitting room for present opening.

The tree was real but it wasn't pine. 'There are no pines here and there's no way I'm spending money importing one,' Letty growled, following his gaze. 'This might not be what you're used to, but it's okay with us.'

It was a small gum tree in a vast pot on wheels. 'We pull it in and pull it out every year,' Letty said while Meg said nothing. 'This year's the last for this tree; she's getting too big. We'll plant her out but there's already a new one coming on to take her place.'

And that made him feel weird as well. The thought of such continuity. A long line of trees, each taking its turn as a Christmas tree before growing to be one of the huge gums that surrounded the farm. Fantastic. And sort of…grounded. Good.

The decorations were great as well, all home-made, some wonderful, some distinctly corny.

'They date from the time Meg arrived here,' Letty said proudly. 'She made paper chains, her mum made the balls and lanterns, then Scotty came along and here's his kindergarten things…'

'Grandma…' Scott said, revolted, and Letty chuckled and tossed him a gift.

It was a sweater. Home knitted. Scott made a truly manful effort to look pleased and the hug he gave his grandma was genuine. He put it on. Red and green stripes. Just the thing…

'For winter,' he said, and Letty beamed with pleasure.

Meg said, 'But take it off before you faint in the heat.'

Scott threw his sister a look of such gratitude that William had trouble not to laugh out loud. As he did with so many of the gifts they were opening, small jokes, trivia, fun.

And then there was a gift in his hands. He stared down at the box—small, flat, red and tied with gold ribbon.

'You've done enough for us,' Meg said softly. 'We can't possibly repay you, but this is the least we can do.'

He opened the box, feeling disoriented, as if he'd been transported to another world. Inside was a certificate, folded neatly.

He read through, trying to make it out.

He'd been given…a part-time dog?

'Scott and I found it on the Internet,' Meg said as he looked up, astounded. 'It's an animal shelter in Manhattan, and it's not far from where you live. This gives you visiting rights. More. What you do is adopt a dog whenever you're in town. If you're based in New York for three months, then you take a dog for three months. You can take her back to the shelter at night if you want, or you can keep her at home, or you can simply take her out for a run each day. Whatever you want. You give your time and the shelter takes over what you can't provide. The only stipulation is that she's still available for permanent adoption. This plan means the shelter can take far more dogs than they could otherwise care for, and they don't have to put them down. But if someone wants to adopt one permanently, then you need to choose another.'

A part-time dog, he thought. Like Ned and Pip and Elinor. His part-time family. Good. Excellent.

So why did it make him feel empty?

Luckily, Scott was filling his silence. 'The dog you've semi-adopted is Sheeba,' he told William. 'Her photograph's in the bottom of the box. She's part greyhound, part Dalmatian. I reckon she should be your first.'

'Because every man needs a dog,' Letty said solidly.

William glanced out towards the kitchen. The dogs weren't permitted in the sitting room. There were five dogs squashed in the doorway, each nose managing to claim an inch of sitting room carpet.

Every man should have a dog. A part-time dog.

He watched as Meg opened yet another extraordinary knitted object and hugged Letty and giggled, and then watched as Scott and Letty were both ordered to open their gifts from Meg together, so they did, and they were bazooka-like machine guns loaded with foam balls. Christmas immediately became a running battle between grandmother and grandson. Who'd have thought Letty had been close to death yesterday, and who'd have ever thought of giving a grandmother a foam ball-shooter?

He looked at Meg and Meg was giggling like a kid—and he thought he was never going to see her again.

He started gathering wrapping paper, and then Letty remembered the turkey and Scott remembered flights.

'Oh, whoops, sorry,' he said, firing a foam ball at Killer, who caught it neatly in his mouth, bit it in two and then looked expectantly for more. 'Killer!'

'Sorry, what?'

'Your flights.' He looked to Meg, as if to confirm he was doing the right thing. 'I checked while you were milking. If you really want to go…'

'What have you found?' Meg asked.

'There's a flight at nine tonight. You could catch the four o'clock train back to Melbourne and take the skybus to the airport. It all fits. Is that okay, Meg?'

'He's used to private cars,' Meg said, not looking at William. 'But it sounds okay.' She rose and headed out to the kitchen after Letty, tossing her words over her shoulder. Still carefully not looking at him. 'Is that okay with you, William? You can have Christmas dinner and we'll drive you to the train.'

'He'll need extra weight allowance after Grandma's pudding,' Scott joked and Letty hooted from the kitchen, but William didn't laugh.

He couldn't see Meg any more. She was behind the kitchen door, but he was willing to bet she didn't laugh either.

'You don't need to come to church,' Meg said, but sitting back at the farmhouse without them seemed unthinkable. So he went and Meg orchestrated things so she sat with Letty and Scott between them. She was wearing another of her new dresses—lilac, simpler than yesterday's, but just as pretty.

Or more pretty. Or maybe it was that he was looking at her more often.

The service was lovely, a tiny community coming together in happiness, belting out beloved Christmas hymns with enthusiasm and as much tunefulness as they could muster. William could only stand for the first two hymns because, some time between the second and the third, Letty leaned against his shoulder and went to sleep. Meg saw why he wasn't standing and she smiled at him, the smile he'd worked with for three years and hadn't noticed, and he thought it was worth holding Letty to receive that smile.

Though, if he'd had a choice... He still would hold Letty, he thought, memories of yesterday's terror flooding back. She was an indomitable old lady and he could see why Meg loved her.

So he sat while the rest of the congregation sang and there were approving looks from many, and curious looks from more, and he thought Meg was going to get the full inquisition after he left.

After he left...

Maybe he could stay a few days more. Make sure Letty was okay. Give Kerrie a few more days off milking.

Get closer to Meg?

She was sharing a song sheet with Scott, and her voice was true and pure. He could hear her through the rest of the congregation—he knew her voice.

He wouldn't hear it again.

He shouldn't be here. This wasn't his place. If he got closer...

He'd hurt her. He didn't know the first thing about family.

He'd go home to his part-time dog, his part-time Foster-Friends role, his full-time career.

What was he doing? Surely he wasn't thinking he could stay here and milk cows for ever?

Maybe he could take Meg with him.

She wouldn't go.

'Collection,' Scott hissed, and he looked at him in incomprehension.

'Money,' Scott said and grinned and William realised he was being handed the collection plate. Everyone in the pew was looking at him. They must have thought he was as sleepy as Letty.

Before he could react, Meg dropped a note into the plate and handed it back to the server. 'He's a bit tight,' she said, in a make-believe whisper which carried through the church. 'He hasn't had any work since before Christmas, you know.'

He stared at her in open-mouthed astonishment and she grinned and then chuckled and Letty stirred against him and opened her eyes.

'Have we sung *O Little Town of Bethlehem* yet?'

'No,' he said, confounded.

'Then why don't we?' she demanded. 'Don't they know our turkey's waiting?'

Dinner came next. Kerrie arrived with her three children and it was hard to know who whooped louder, the children or Letty. Far too much food was consumed. The pudding flamed magnificently. Crackers were pulled. Silly jokes were read. Meg checked her watch for about the hundredth time and finally said, 'It's time to go.'

'It is,' William said. 'You'll drive me to the station?'

'I'll drive you,' Letty said with alacrity and grinned. 'Meg can do the washing-up.'

'Let Meg take him, Grandma,' Scott said with rare insight. 'She'll want to say goodbye.'

'I want to say goodbye,' Letty retorted.

Scott said, 'Grandma,' in a meaningful voice and Letty gave a theatrical sigh and started clearing the table. But she wasn't exactly martyred. Kerrie and Scott were helping clear. Kerrie would stay on for milking—they'd organised that at some time over pudding. It'd only take Meg twenty minutes to take William to the station. Ten minutes there, ten minutes back and life would go on without him.

As it should.

He'd already packed his bag. He rose from the still laden table and felt... empty.

'Thank you,' he said simply and Letty looked at him as if he was a sandwich short of a picnic.

'Thank us? After what you've done for us?'

'I'll send you pictures of my car,' Scott said shyly. 'As it takes shape.'

'I'd like that.'

There was nothing else to say. Meg was already at the door, keys in her hand.

Ready to move on?

CHAPTER ELEVEN

WHY didn't he speak? The tension seemed unbearable. Thankfully, the station was only ten minutes' drive, otherwise she'd explode. Or something. She flicked on the radio and there were the inevitable Christmas carols. William flicked them straight off.

'What's wrong with my carols?' she demanded, trying to sound offended.

'I'm crossing the time line tonight. I'm facing another twenty-four hours of Christmas. Enough is enough.'

'Two Christmases in a row. How appalling.' So much for offended. She knew she sounded miserable.

'My Christmas isn't like your Christmas,' he told her. 'Two of my normal Christmases would be appalling.'

'Will you see your parents?'

'No.'

'You should. Even the media says they're lonely. Call them.'

'You're telling me how to run my life?'

'I forgot,' she said, suddenly contrite. 'I'm still employed. I shouldn't tell you anything.'

'But when you're not employed?'

'When I'm not employed I won't be anywhere near you,' she whispered. There was more silence and then, thankfully, they arrived. She pulled up beside the platform—it really was in the middle of nowhere. But this was where she had to leave him.

'Here you are,' she managed, feeling ill. 'The train will be here in six minutes.'

He looked around him in doubt. 'How do I know you're right with your timetable?'

'Trust me.'

'Trust you to leave me standing on a platform in the middle of nowhere, waiting for a train, when I only have your word for it that it'll come?'

She sighed. 'Okay, I'll wait. Sir. Do you want me to carry your bag onto the station?'

'No,' he said. 'Meg…'

'We need to be on the station. If the driver can't see us from a way ahead he won't stop.' She headed onto the platform, leaving him to follow.

He followed.

More silence. They stood side by side in the middle of nowhere and he tried to think of something to say. So many things, but none of them suitable. None of them possible.

'Reconsider your job,' he said at last and she shook her head.

'I can't.'

'Because I kissed you?'

'I believe I resigned before that.'

'Because I wanted to kiss you, then? And because when I did kiss you, it was wonderful?'

'William, I can't cope with an affair,' she said simply. 'And I can't cope with loving my boss.'

'Loving…' The word made him feel as if he'd been punched.

'I don't, of course,' she said hastily. 'It's just that I might. Given time and enough…heat.' There was a faint speck on the horizon, a distant rumble and they both knew the train was on its way. 'So…so it's been fabulous. I've had the best time working for you and I can't begin to thank you for what you've done for my family this Christmas.'

'There's no need to thank me.' Did he take her hands or did she take his? He didn't know. All he did know was that suddenly they were linked. The train was growing closer and she was just…*here.*

He was holding Meg. Not Miss Jardine. He was definitely holding Meg. And he knew what he most wanted to say.

'Come with me,' he said urgently, and her eyes widened.

'What?'

'To New York. You could have a second Christmas too.'

'I've had Christmas.' The train was closer now. The driver had seen them and was starting to slow.

'I want you to come.'

'And leave Letty and Scott? Ring them up and say sorry, I won't be home for tea, can you get someone to cover the milking?' She sounded a little hysterical. Panicked. Her hands tugged back, but he didn't let her go. 'What are you saying? Christmas in New York… That's crazy.'

He knew it was. 'Crazy or not, I mean it.'

She met his gaze square on, and the flare of panic settled. 'No,' she said, sounding sure. 'My place is here. As yours is in Manhattan. Or Hong Kong. Or London. Wherever your business takes you. And here's your train. Say hello to Sheeba for me.'

'Sheeba?'

'Your part-time dog,' she chided and he stared down at her and thought—part-time dog, part-time life; he so didn't want to leave this woman.

But the alternative?

She couldn't go with him. There wasn't an alternative.

'Goodbye, William,' she said gently and pushed his hands

a little, pushing him to let her go. Only the train hadn't quite stopped yet and his hold on her tightened.

'Goodbye, Meg.' There was a blast from the train's horn, as if the driver was saying get on fast; the train surely didn't want to waste time sitting at this windswept, sunburned country railway siding. No one would want to waste time here. Least of all him.

He had to leave.

But how could he leave when he was holding Meg?

He must.

He looked down into her eyes for one last time, and then, because there was no way he couldn't, he pulled her tight against him. He cupped her chin, he tilted her face—and then he kissed her.

It was a fast kiss, fast by necessity as the train had now stopped. But still the kiss was strong and searching, and it ached to be more. For one precious moment she yielded against him, her mouth opened under his and she melted. Her body moulded against his and she was crushed against him.

Meg.

But the doors of the train were sliding open and the conductor was stepping onto the platform.

'All aboard,' he snapped, straight at them, and there was no avoiding the inevitable. For one last moment Meg clung and he held, and then she was standing back and there was nothing he could do but lift his bag and board the train.

She drove home feeling sick. Life as she knew it was over.

Well, that was a stupid thing to think. She had cows to look forward to. And finding a local job. Plus there was a rather nice young farmer who'd been interested before she'd left to take the McMaster job. Letty told her every time she came home that he was still single. Maybe she could drum up some enthusiasm.

Only she'd taken the job with William for a reason and the reason still stood. She loved the farm, but it wasn't enough.

She'd adored working for William. For Mr McMaster.

For William. He could never be Mr McMaster again. She knew that. He was too cute, too warm-hearted, too…hot.

And too needy. See, there was the problem. What really hurt—or, if she was honest, what hurt almost as much as missing him—was the thought of him going back to his sterile life in Manhattan. Sure, he had his part-time kids and now he had his part-time dog. Sure, he thought he was happy. He was rich and confident and a powerful figure in the world's economy.

But he wouldn't call his parents and she guessed they wouldn't call him. He'd probably call one of his Cool-To-Be-Seen-With women to fill in the gaps in his life, and that made her think dark thoughts about life in general and Cool-To-Be-Seen-With women in particular. She dredged up an image of the erstwhile Sarah, and imagined the picture as a dartboard.

How childish was that?

She *was* being childish. But there was more behind what she was feeling than childishness, and she knew what it was.

For she'd fallen in love. Some time over the last two days, she'd fallen hard. Maybe it had been latent, waiting in the wings to strike when the time was right. Maybe she'd been in love with W S McMaster for years; she just hadn't known it.

And he was going home alone and she felt sick—and sad for him as well as for her. He'd go back to the life he knew and she didn't envy him one bit. He might be rich and powerful but she had Scotty and Letty and the dogs.

She didn't have William.

He'd asked her to go with him. How crazy was that? Oh,

but she'd wanted to. To board the train and leave, flying to Manhattan with William, stepping into his life…

His part-time life. For she was under no illusions as to what an affair with William would be. She'd made arrangements for too many such affairs in the past. Glorious indulgence and then mutual parting, no hard feelings.

She pulled the car off the road and got out. She walked round the car, then round again. It was no use going back to the farm until she had her head in order.

William was gone, and she had to move on. She had to walk into the kitchen at home and be cheerful.

Right. One more round of the car, or maybe two, and she could do it.

She must.

He heaved his bag up onto the luggage rack and he thought for the first time—he *had* been preoccupied until now—that his bag was heavier than usual. And, almost as he thought it, the zip burst open.

His luggage was quality. Zips did not burst.

Nor did plastic bags and plastic containers spill out onto the floor of the train.

But, over Christmas, W S McMaster had become William, and someone had packed leftovers in William's bag. The transparent containers held turkey, plum pudding, grapes, cherries, chocolates and more. There was also a plastic bottle labelled Brandy Sauce.

Meg would never do this. It must have been Letty. Meg was far too sensible to pack him leftovers.

Or was she?

He'd get rid of it at the airport, he thought, gathering the containers while bemused passengers watched. He travelled first class. Leftovers compared to the airline's best haute cuisine?

But then he thought, this was Letty's cooking and Jenny's cooking. Maybe there was even Meg's cooking in there somewhere. She'd definitely stirred the pudding.

Maybe he wouldn't get rid of it.

He started shoving the containers back into his bag and realised there was something deeper. He delved and found…a bazooka. Complete with foam bullets. It was the same as the ones Letty and Scott had found in their stockings, orange, purple and gold. A note was attached.

To William. I had huge trouble finding you one of these at short notice but I knew you'd be jealous of Letty and Scott so, with Mickey's help, here's your very own. I thought it might cheer you up when you reach home. You and Pip and Ned can play with it in Central Park. Just don't take it on board your plane as hand luggage. You could get into Very Serious Trouble. Love Meg.

Ridiculous.

But… He *had* been jealous this morning as Letty and Scott had shot each other. As if he was on the outside looking in.

Pip and Ned would think this was cool. *He* thought it was cool. He wanted to try it out now.

Or not. Mature businessmen did not shoot foam bazookas on trains.

He read the note again.

Love Meg.

Don't go there.

He stowed the bazooka. He managed to get his bag refastened, and finally sank into his seat.

The train was almost empty. Of course. It was Christmas night. Who'd be travelling tonight except people going from one family to another?

There was a young mother in the seat opposite, hugging

her baby. Maybe she wasn't going from one family to another. She looked wan and tear-stained.

The W S McMaster of Friday would hardly have noticed. But now... 'Are you okay?' he asked.

'I...yes. Thank you.' She managed a watery smile; she clearly wanted to talk. 'My husband's working on an off-shore oil rig so we can save a deposit for a house. We only have one week together a month. It's only for a year but I hate being a part-time family. And I have to go back to my parents tonight... Night's my favourite time. When the day's over, snuggling down and talking about it... Oh, I miss him. I love him so much.'

She sniffed and blew her nose and there was nothing he could say to make her feel better. He retrieved some of his leftover chocolates. They shared their chocolate and their si-lence, and neither of them was happy.

I love him so much...

There was a lot in that statement to avoid thinking about. He decided he'd think about the rest.

Night's my favourite time...

He hated Christmas night. Christmas Day was usually bearable—there were always social functions, and last year he'd had Pip and Ned. Only at the end...

When the day's over, snuggling down and talking about it...

That was what was missing. He'd never figured it out. How could he miss what he'd never known?

Christmas night alone... He always did Christmas night alone.

Maybe he'd be home in time to see Pip and Ned.

He checked his phone and then remembered. No reception.

'You can ring when we go through towns,' the girl told him. 'Only you need to talk fast.'

When the day's over, snuggling down and talking about it...

The last twenty-four hours had been huge. Who could he talk about it with?

They were approaching a town. Sure enough, reception bars appeared on his cellphone. He rang Manhattan. Elinor. She answered on the first ring.

'What's wrong?' She sounded breathless and he realised it was one in the morning back home. Night-time.

When the day's over, snuggling down and talking about it...

'I'm sorry,' he said. 'I've woken you.'

'Oh, Mr McMaster, it's you,' she said. 'No, I was just stuffing stockings, so you didn't wake me. I'm glad you rang. I have such good news.'

'You do?'

'The children... Their mother's finally agreed to their adoption. The agency contacted me this morning. There's a couple... They lost their children in a car accident five years ago and they so want a family. They sound lovely and there's grandmas and grandpas; everything these children most need. So tomorrow, after Christmas lunch, they're coming to visit. It's only first contact, but oh, they sound nice. These children so need a family.'

'They do,' he said and somehow he managed to keep his voice from sounding bereft. Bereft? Of all the stupid sensations...

And Elinor heard it—he knew she did. 'There's so many needy children out there,' she said, her voice growing sombre. 'You know that. There's always more to be looked after.'

And he heard her pain as well. She'd be giving up these children and moving on. 'Oh, Elinor.' She loved with all her heart. You didn't love without hurting. Where had he learned that? Was he just starting?

'Yeah, it hurts,' she said across his thoughts, and he could almost see her steeling herself. 'But, if you don't love, then you might as well stop living. This family live right nearby so we'll see each other in the park. So how about you? Will we see you tomorrow? I mean, today?'

'My flight won't get in until late.'

'Oh, the children will be disappointed,' she said, but in a tone that said not too disappointed; they were about to meet their new mommy and daddy. What more did children need for Christmas?

'So you'll be flying all Christmas,' she said. 'I'm so sorry.'

'There's no need to be sorry,' he said, startled.

'Well, there is,' she said, and she sounded truly concerned. 'It's time you stayed put. I know you're important and I know you're busy but you have a good heart, Mr McMaster, and it's time you found somewhere to park it. I've done my share of parking in my time, but have you? You need to find somewhere you can leave it for good.'

The train had streamed through the town and out the other side. Reception was starting to break up. He could barely hear.

Maybe it was just as well, William thought. What sort of advice was this? He wished her Merry Christmas, but he didn't hear a response. He clicked off his phone and stared out of the window. Trying not to replay her words.

'Bad news?' the young mother asked.

'I…no. Good news, really.'

'You don't look like it was good news.'

'It's okay.'

He wanted to tell her about it. Only…if he told her…how could he make it sound like good news? She'd guess how he felt, he thought, as Elinor had guessed. As Meg would guess?

He wanted to tell Meg.

When the day's over, snuggling down and talking about it...

Such a thing wasn't for him. For a McMaster to...snuggle... Unthinkable.

He stared out at the sparse Australian landscape, so unlike Manhattan, and he thought of his family—the McMaster dynasty. Damaged people all. Deeply unhappy. Poisoned by wealth and by social expectations. Unhappy unions had created unhappy children, and on it went, for generation after generation, spreading outward.

How could he ask someone to join such a family?

He couldn't. He'd sworn he never would. But, if not...

The thought came from nowhere, and it started as a jumble. A Christmas tree with decorations from childhood. Letty's mango trifle. Cows and dogs. Gumboots parked at the back door. Meg's laughter...

Crazy Santa legs. Scott amid a jumble of Mini parts. The feel of Meg against him in the emergency room.

This was a family so unlike his own it was unbelievable, and the jumbled thought unravelled, settled and finally left a clear thought that was amazing.

If his family was unworkable...

Maybe he could join another?

The conductor was coming through now, checking tickets and, before he could take the thought any further, he found himself asking, 'Is there another train tonight?'

'To where?'

'To where I got on.'

'To Tandaroit? You have to be joking. Once a day to Tandaroit. Next train leaves tomorrow night from Melbourne.'

'Do you want to go back?' the woman across the way asked as the conductor moved on.

'Maybe,' William said, feeling dazed.

'To the girl you were kissing on the station?'

And there it was, front and centre. The girl he'd been kissing on the station.

'Who is she?' the woman asked and he managed a smile.

'She was Miss Jardine,' he said softly. 'But now…her name is Meg.'

CHAPTER TWELVE

MEG liked Christmas night, or she always had. Christmas was huge, busy, noisy, fun, and it left her happy. Even the first appalling Christmas after the accident, she and Letty had managed to make it fun and she'd slept that night feeling just a little bit optimistic about the future.

So why wasn't she feeling optimistic now?

Kerrie stayed and helped with the milking while Letty and Scott cleaned up inside and minded the children. After tea, they loaded the sleeping children into Kerrie's car and bade them goodnight. Kerrie drove off and Meg found herself feeling jealous. Kerrie would be snuggling the children into bed.

Um… Kerrie was a struggling single mother who worked herself raw. Was she jealous because she had babies?

Was she jealous of what they represented?

Scott and Letty went to bed, tired and happy after what they decreed had been an awesome Christmas. 'We should invite William every year,' Scott said sleepily and Meg felt even more bereft.

The dogs had eaten too many leftovers. They were asleep; useless as company.

She went across to the home paddock to talk to Millicent, but Millicent was snoozing as well.

She walked back to the house, kicking stones, disconsolate. Santa was still waving back and forth in his chimney.

'I wonder if I can shoot him down with one of the bazookas?' she asked herself but she couldn't dredge up a smile.

She didn't want to smile. She wanted to wallow.

She climbed into her pyjamas and went to bed. She thumped her pillows for a while, then gave up and headed back into the kitchen to pour herself the last of the eggnog. She stared into its depths and then carefully tipped it down the sink.

'Let's not drown our sorrows here,' she told herself. 'We need to be nice and sober to read the Job Vacancy ads tomorrow.'

She sniffed. 'Ooh, who's maudlin? And I haven't even drunk my eggnog.'

William would be back in Melbourne now. She looked at her watch. No. William would be in the sky.

She glanced out of the window at the stars beyond. Nothing and nothing and nothing.

And...something. A tiny light, growing brighter.

It was a small plane, she thought, low in the east. Some private charter, going places now the restrictions were lifted. Good for them.

The light was getting brighter. Brighter still. And the sound...

Not a plane, then. A helicopter.

Closer still. Low and fast.

Who...?

And then she thought...

No.

Yes?

This was stupid. She was imagining things. Maybe there'd been an accident somewhere close and this was an air transfer. That'd be it.

But it was over their land now. Hovering. Lights were beaming down.

It'd panic the cows.

But, even as she thought it, she realised it wasn't hovering over the cow pastures. The paddock underneath was at the eastern extremity of the property, where the hay had been slashed only yesterday.

Whoever was in the chopper knew the paddock was bare. Knew the paddock was safe.

It'd be… It'd be…

She daren't think who it'd be.

It wouldn't be William.

But the chopper was on her land.

The dogs had heard. Killer was at the kitchen door, his head to one side, listening.

'I'll take you with me,' she told him, and then as the rest of the pack appeared, she nodded. 'Okay, maybe I do need protection. Let's all go and investigate.'

He stood in the paddock and he thought, whoa, it's a long way to the house. He knew he couldn't scare the cows; he knew this paddock would be a safe place to land, but still…

'Where's a limousine when you need it?' The pilot was enjoying himself. Yes, he'd been pulled away from his family Christmas, but he'd had his Christmas dinner and the bonus he'd been promised made him very happy indeed. 'Maybe I could take you over the house and lower you on a rope,' he told him, grinning, and William thought, where's the respect? He'd made the mistake of chatting to Steve about his family, and look where it got him.

And then he saw Letty's wagon bumping across the paddocks and he stopped thinking about Steve—he stopped thinking of anything but Meg.

Was it Meg? The car came to a halt, the driver's door

opened, but, before he could see who it was five dogs tumbled out, enveloping him in a sea of canine ecstasy.

He'd been at the farm for three days. By the dogs' reaction, they were his lifelong friends and he'd been gone for years.

He kind of liked it. But still... Hopefully, Meg was behind them. He managed to shove the dogs aside. The pack descended on Steve, who backed into his cockpit. The dogs jumped right up after him. Hopefully, the machine was hard to start, otherwise they risked flight by dog. Whatever, William was too busy looking at Meg to do anything about it.

For she was here.

She was wearing...pyjamas? Pink silk with tiny stars and moons all over. Silver stars. His sense of unreality deepened. Her hair was messed as if she'd been asleep. She looked rumpled and sexy and so fabulous he wanted to scoop her into his arms right then and there.

Think of something to say, Stupid, he told himself but he was having trouble. Tonight had made sense to him at the planning stage. Now he was having trouble getting started.

'You had to bring the dogs,' he managed, as a muffled grunt emerged from the cockpit.

'Anyone could be landing in our hay paddock. On the chance that you could be enemy alien cow poachers...'

'You came wearing pyjamas?'

'I have a loaded bazooka under these pyjamas.'

He eyed the pyjamas. They were silky and clinging and...

No. Don't think of what might or might not be under those pyjamas. Definitely not a bazooka.

What to say? He gazed at Meg, at her adorably confused face, at her wonderful stars and moons, at her dishevelled hair. This was Meg, the woman he loved with all his heart, and he knew he had to go forward.

The woman he loved with all his heart...

When had he figured this out? Just then, he thought. He'd known he had to come. He'd planned to come. But now, looking at her, he knew for sure.

All those corny movies he'd watched as a lonely child… they were right. Throw your hat into the ring.

Jump.

'I had to come back for you,' he said simply, his gaze not leaving her face.

'I said I couldn't come with you,' she whispered, sounding awed.

'You don't need to come. I didn't come back to fetch you. I came back to be with you.'

'P…pardon?'

'I came back because I love you,' he said, strongly now, more sure. 'I came back because when it came down to it I couldn't leave.'

'You love me?' She said it wonderingly, and he knew the alien thing was still in her mind. She said it as if his words were some sort of fantasy that had no connection to reality.

It was up to him to make her see this was real. That this was true.

'I do love you.' It was as serious as any wedding vow. He took a step towards her but she held up her hands as if to ward him off. As if she was afraid.

Behind him, Steve was still surrounded by dogs. He couldn't be holding five collars, yet the dogs were all still. It was as if they sensed how important this was.

Was this important to a chopper pilot? To dogs?

Why not? It was the whole world to him.

'Meg, I need to know,' he said roughly, because he couldn't bear to wait a moment longer. 'When you talked about loving… Did you mean it? That you could love me?'

'I might,' she whispered, and his world settled. Things were falling into place that he'd never realised were out of kilter until now. That he'd known this woman for three long years and not loved her... How could he have been so blind?

How could he waste another moment? It was killing him not to take her into his arms but he knew he shouldn't.

Do not rush this.

As if falling in love in three days, hiring a helicopter in the middle of the night, telling her he wanted her right now, wasn't rushing things.

Okay, do not rush this even more.

So say it. Lay the whole plan on the line.

'I can move here,' he said and Meg's face froze.

'Here?'

'It's not impossible.'

'I think I need to sit.'

'Can I hold you up?'

'Not until I figure what you're talking about.'

'My plans.'

'I like plans,' she said faintly. 'Okay, talk.'

So he talked. 'I'll explain fast,' he said, and it had to be fast because if he didn't hold her soon he'd go up in smoke. 'I propose to base myself here. No, wrong, I propose we base ourselves here, because I need you, Meg, in business, in every facet of my life. You're smart and intuitive and funny and I want you with me every step of the way. So what I'd really like is to build here, set up headquarters here. Keep the farm but add to it. We'd need a helicopter pad. I fancy a swimming pool. And I bet a gymnasium would really help Scott.'

'Scott...'

'He's part of it. He's part of your life. Family.'

'William...'

'I know,' he said hurriedly, afraid to stop, afraid of how she'd respond. 'It's just it was a really long train ride back to Melbourne, and making plans is what I'm principally good at. I thought we could restore the old cottage on the other side of the dairy and ask Kerrie if she'd consider living here. Letty told me it was a dream of yours and it sounds good to me. That means we'd always have a milker on hand. Then… maybe we could employ a nanny…'

'A nanny,' she said, astonished.

'For Kerrie's kids,' he said hurriedly. 'And for…for who-ever else might come along. That means you and I can travel, whenever we wish. There's so much… It'll take us years to sort it out, but we will. We can. If we want to. If you want to. What…what do you think?'

There was a long, long pause. The enemy alien cow poacher was still in the back of her mind, he thought, but slowly, slowly, he watched her expression change. She was searching his face and what she saw seemed to change things.

'I think…' she whispered, but then her voice firmed. 'I think I'd never leave our kids with a nanny,' she said, and suddenly the woman in the pink silk pyjamas was smiling.

His heart gave a leap. *I'd never leave our kids…* There were all sorts of assumptions in that statement, and he liked them all.

'How many kids would you like?' he asked tenderly.

'William!'

Maybe he had to throw in a few more inducements. Maybe he still didn't have it right. How to talk of love… It seemed so fragile—and all he had was words. Not now.

'You know, Letty and Scotty could travel with us too, if they like,' he said hurriedly. 'They could see Manhattan. And London and Hong Kong. I think they'd like it. But I'm serious about only travelling when I must.' He hesitated. 'You know, I didn't get this right. My parents taught me personal stuff was a disaster so I buried myself in work. But you…you enjoy what you do for me, yes?'

'I love it,' she said simply.

'Yet you love the farm.'

'Yes.'

'As I like pulling silencers off cars.'

'Do you?'

'I do,' he said and it was a vow. She was looking at him very strangely but he'd started—he had to explain. And he was struggling to explain it to himself.

Words… Find the right words, he told himself. Get it right.

Say the love word.

'I've been thinking…if I could mix grease guns with business, then maybe I could mix loving in there somewhere as well,' he tried, but it didn't sound right.

'In the spare bits?'

'No,' he said, sure of himself on this one. 'In all my bits. In my business. In my spare time, in my hobbies, in my dreams. I want loving in all of it. Meg, I want you.'

She looked stunned. She looked star-struck. 'You're truly serious?'

And there was only one answer to that. 'I've never been more serious about anything in my life,' he said simply. 'No matter what happens, at the end of every day of my life I want to lie in bed with you.'

'And…talk?' she managed, and there was the beginning of laughter in her lovely eyes.

'Or anything else that might occur to us,' he told her, smiling, loving her with all his heart, and suddenly she chuckled, a lovely deep ripple of wonder, and he thought he might just have got this right.

'So will you marry me?' he asked, for what else was there to say?

She gasped. 'You want to marry me?'

'Yes.' Then… 'But I do have a problem,' he was forced to admit. 'Try as I might, Christmas night is not a time to buy a ring.'

'Not?' she said and she laced her voice with such a depth of disappointment that he wasn't sure where the chuckle ended and sincerity began.

Aargh. He had everything right except this. But then Killer took a leap from the chopper and lumbered over. Dangling from his collar was his dog tag. It was a ring—of sorts.

'Excuse me, Killer,' he said and flicked off the collar and removed the tag. 'Can I borrow this until the shops reopen?'

'I don't believe this,' Meg said faintly.

'We need to organise new tags, anyway,' William said, refastening the collar. 'I'm shipping Sheeba out here as soon as I possibly can.'

'You're shipping Sheeba…'

'I figure you have one dog; Letty has two and Scott has two. When I decided to stay, I took out my Christmas card and stared at the picture of Sheeba and thought—how could I turn my back on such a fine gift? But I'm not doing part-time anything any more, so she gets to be full-time. I'm hoping she likes being a farm dog, but how could she not?' And then, because this seemed as good a time as any, he dropped on one knee and held out the dog tag. 'So, Miss Jardine…'

'Meg,' she said sharply.

'Meg,' he said, suitably chastened. 'My love.'

'That's much better.' She was smiling mistily down at him. *'My love* is way better than Meg.'

'Hey!' It was a piercing shout and he turned, groaning. But the shout and the associated rumble couldn't be ignored.

For it was Letty and Scott, bouncing over the paddocks towards them on the ancient farm tractor. 'Don't you dare propose until we get there,' Letty yelled in a voice that was truly scary.

'Am I so obvious?' he demanded of his love and his love chuckled and behind them Steve laughed and Killer started barking.

'My love...' he started urgently, but Meg put her finger on his lips and hushed him. She tugged him up and she smiled.

'I wouldn't have it any other way,' she whispered. 'In front of witnesses.'

'You have to be joking.'

'You've been a loner all your life, William McMaster. No more.'

So he waited. With a promise like that, a man could wait. He waited until Letty and Scott were in full earshot and they'd introduced themselves to Steve and they were holding the dogs back and then Letty said, 'Okay, get on with it.'

And William, who was feeling absurdly self-conscious, suddenly thought no.

'No,' he said.

'No?' Meg said.

'Steve, how many does that chopper hold?'

'Six,' Steve said.

'Three people and five dogs?'

'At a push.'

'Then there are free chopper flights on offer,' he said. 'Starting now. You guys can watch, but from above. Take it or leave it. Witnesses from above, but not right here.'

'Oh, cool,' Scotty said, high with excitement. 'Come on, Grandma, who wants to listen to a soppy proposal when we can ride in a chopper? And it is,' he added conscientiously, 'their business anyway.'

So, before Letty knew what she was about, her grandson had bundled her into the chopper. The dogs were tossed up after. The doors were clanged shut and the chopper rose into the night sky.

But not very far. William might have intended that Steve take them far away. Steve had other ideas.

The chopper simply hovered. Its downlight nailed them.

'You were saying?' Meg yelled at the top of her lungs,

laughing, and William thought he was never, ever going to be able to do this better than he could right now. He was standing in the middle of a hay paddock. A helicopter was practically blasting him to bits with its down-draught. The moon was high in the night sky, and over at the house Santa's legs moved steadily back and forth, back and forth, back and forth.

'Happy Christmas,' he shouted, and he tried again for the third time. Third time lucky? 'Will you marry me?'

'What?' The sound of the chopper was deafening.

'With this ring, I thee wed?' he shouted back and he placed the tag on her finger and he scooped her up and lifted her high into his arms, holding her hard against his heart. And finally he kissed her as he needed to kiss her, as she needed to be kissed, as he intended to kiss her for the rest of her life.

'I'll give you diamonds,' he yelled when they could finally bear to pull apart.

'Who needs diamonds?' Meg said lovingly. He could barely hear her words but he knew what her lips were saying. It was what his heart was saying.

'Merry Christmas, my love,' she told him. 'Diamonds or not, I just need you.'

* * * * *

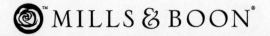
MILLS & BOON®

NOVEMBER 2010 HARDBACK TITLES

ROMANCE

The Dutiful Wife	Penny Jordan
His Christmas Virgin	Carole Mortimer
Public Marriage, Private Secrets	Helen Bianchin
Forbidden or For Bedding?	Julia James
The Twelve Nights of Christmas	Sarah Morgan
In Christofides' Keeping	Abby Green
The Italian's Blushing Gardener	Christina Hollis
The Socialite and the Cattle King	Lindsay Armstrong
Tabloid Affair, Secretly Pregnant!	Mira Lyn Kelly
Maharaja's Mistress	Susan Stephens
Christmas with her Boss	Marion Lennox
Firefighter's Doorstep Baby	Barbara McMahon
Daddy by Christmas	Patricia Thayer
Christmas Magic on the Mountain	Melissa McClone
A FAIRYTALE CHRISTMAS	Susan Meier & Barbara Wallace
The Soldier's Untamed Heart	Nikki Logan
Dr Zinetti's Snowkissed Bride	Sarah Morgan
The Christmas Baby Bump	Lynne Marshall

HISTORICAL

Courting Miss Vallois	Gail Whitiker
Reprobate Lord, Runaway Lady	Isabelle Goddard
The Bride Wore Scandal	Helen Dickson

MEDICAL™

Christmas in Bluebell Cove	Abigail Gordon
The Village Nurse's Happy-Ever-After	Abigail Gordon
The Most Magical Gift of All	Fiona Lowe
Christmas Miracle: A Family	Dianne Drake

1010 Gen Std LP

MILLS & BOON

NOVEMBER 2010 LARGE PRINT TITLES

ROMANCE

A Night, A Secret...A Child	Miranda Lee
His Untamed Innocent	Sara Craven
The Greek's Pregnant Lover	Lucy Monroe
The Mélendez Forgotten Marriage	Melanie Milburne
Australia's Most Eligible Bachelor	Margaret Way
The Bridesmaid's Secret	Fiona Harper
Cinderella: Hired by the Prince	Marion Lennox
The Sheikh's Destiny	Melissa James

HISTORICAL

The Earl's Runaway Bride	Sarah Mallory
The Wayward Debutante	Sarah Elliott
The Laird's Captive Wife	Joanna Fulford

MEDICAL™

The Surgeon's Miracle	Caroline Anderson
Dr Di Angelo's Baby Bombshell	Janice Lynn
Newborn Needs a Dad	Dianne Drake
His Motherless Little Twins	Dianne Drake
Wedding Bells for the Village Nurse	Abigail Gordon
Her Long-Lost Husband	Josie Metcalfe

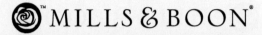

MILLS & BOON

DECEMBER 2010 HARDBACK TITLES

ROMANCE

Naive Bride, Defiant Wife	Lynne Graham
Nicolo: The Powerful Sicilian	Sandra Marton
Stranded, Seduced...Pregnant	Kim Lawrence
Shock: One-Night Heir	Melanie Milburne
Innocent Virgin, Wild Surrender	Anne Mather
Her Last Night of Innocence	India Grey
Captured and Crowned	Janette Kenny
Buttoned-Up Secretary, British Boss	Susanne James
Surf, Sea and a Sexy Stranger	Heidi Rice
Wild Nights with her Wicked Boss	Nicola Marsh
Mistletoe and the Lost Stiletto	Liz Fielding
Rescued by his Christmas Angel	Cara Colter
Angel of Smoky Hollow	Barbara McMahon
Christmas at Candlebark Farm	Michelle Douglas
The Cinderella Bride	Barbara Wallace
Single Father, Surprise Prince!	Raye Morgan
A Christmas Knight	Kate Hardy
The Nurse Who Saved Christmas	Janice Lynn

HISTORICAL

Lady Arabella's Scandalous Marriage	Carole Mortimer
Dangerous Lord, Seductive Miss	Mary Brendan
Bound to the Barbarian	Carol Townend
Bought: The Penniless Lady	Deborah Hale

MEDICAL™

St Piran's: The Wedding of The Year	Caroline Anderson
St Piran's: Rescuing Pregnant Cinderella	Carol Marinelli
The Midwife's Christmas Miracle	Jennifer Taylor
The Doctor's Society Sweetheart	Lucy Clark

MILLS & BOON

DECEMBER 2010 LARGE PRINT TITLES

ROMANCE

The Pregnancy Shock — Lynne Graham
Falco: The Dark Guardian — Sandra Marton
One Night...Nine-Month Scandal — Sarah Morgan
The Last Kolovsky Playboy — Carol Marinelli
Doorstep Twins — Rebecca Winters
The Cowboy's Adopted Daughter — Patricia Thayer
SOS: Convenient Husband Required — Liz Fielding
Winning a Groom in 10 Dates — Cara Colter

HISTORICAL

Rake Beyond Redemption — Anne O'Brien
A Thoroughly Compromised Lady — Bronwyn Scott
In the Master's Bed — Blythe Gifford
Bought: The Penniless Lady — Deborah Hale

MEDICAL™

The Midwife and the Millionaire — Fiona McArthur
From Single Mum to Lady — Judy Campbell
Knight on the Children's Ward — Carol Marinelli
Children's Doctor, Shy Nurse — Molly Evans
Hawaiian Sunset, Dream Proposal — Joanna Neil
Rescued: Mother and Baby — Anne Fraser

Discover Pure Reading Pleasure with

**Visit the Mills & Boon website for all
the latest in romance**

 Buy all the latest
releases, backlist
and eBooks

 Find out more
about our authors
and their books

 Join our community
and chat to authors
and other readers

 Free online reads
from your favourite
authors

 Win with our
fantastic online
competitions

 Sign up for our
free monthly
eNewsletter

 Tell us what you
think by signing up to
our reader panel

 Rate and review
books with our star
system

www.millsandboon.co.uk

 Follow us at twitter.com/millsandboonuk

Become a fan at facebook.com/romancehq